I0586034

Crush

S.R. Silcox

Juggernaut Books PL

Crush

S R Silcox

CRUSH

Copyright © S R Silcox, 2015

First published 2015

Published by Juggernaut Books PL

Email: mail@srsilcox.com

URL: http://www.srsilcox.com

All rights reserved. This book or any portion thereof may not be reproduced or used in any manner whatsoever without the express written permission of the author except for the use of brief quotations in a book review.

This is a work of fiction. Name, characters, places and incidents are a product of the author's imagination. Any resemblance to actual persons, events or locales is entirely coincidental.

Crush

Silcox, S R

Third Edition

Cover designed by GetCovers

Paperback ISBN: 978-0-6482991-2-7

For my family and my cousins, who gave me the best childhood anyone could have imagined.

One

PEOPLE WHO've never experienced a cane fire wonder what all the fuss is about, and then they see one, and they know. A cane fire starts off slow, burning around the edges, the fire creeping into the lower part of the cane, and then it roars up into the tops of the stalks making the night glow orange. Suddenly, just as quickly as it roars to life, it's gone, and all that's left is the black snow - the burned cane trash - falling silently back to the ground. It was the sweetest smell Tess Copeland had ever known, like Gran's kitchen after she'd made toffee, and it was her favourite part of summer.

Tonight's fire was the last one for the season, except for the small block she and Pop had grown for the Crush Festival, and Tess's job was to keep an eye on any big embers coming down still alight, just in case they dropped into the festival block and set it off. With everyone concentrating on the block they were burning, if the festival block caught, there'd be no putting it out. Especially with the dry heat and westerlies they'd had that day.

Tess was sitting on the tailgate of her Pop's ute, her spray pack full of water beside her, watching as Lonny and Pete and some of the other farmers from around Chesterfield lit up the block. In the initial stages, it was quiet as Lonny and Pete walked in opposite directions with their drip torches lighting up the bottom of the cane. A couple of other farmers would be doing the same thing from the other side.

Pop was standing on the eastern corner closest to where the old farm ute was parked, talking to Gary Evans from up the road. Probably about the lack of rain, and most likely about the council elections coming up next year. Gary never missed an opportunity to put in a good word for his wife, who'd been a councillor in Chesterfield for close to fifteen years.

Lonny and Pete were about halfway around the block when the fire crackled to life. Orange flames crept toward the centre of the cane and licked their way up the tall cane stalks, singeing the loose leaves as it went. Gary Evans uncrossed his arms, picked up his fire rake, and walked with Pop to the edge of the cane. Pop nodded at Tess as he passed, and Pete's brother and nephew rode past on their motorbikes, heading for the far side. They were always the last to arrive at a fire, and the last to leave after the beer and sandwiches that Gran put on were gone, but they worked hard so no-one seemed to care. Pete's nephew saluted Tess as he hurtled past, standing tall on the footrests, whooping as he fish-tailed around the corner and out of sight.

Tess pushed off the ute, heaved the spray pack onto her back and, adjusting her cap on her head, walked over to the track between the burning block and the festival block and turned her eyes to the sky.

Within minutes, the fire was roaring up into the centre of the cane, throwing flames high into the air and spewing black smoke. Tess kept a careful eye on a few big pieces of trash as they pin-wheeled down from the sky, but they were out before they hit the ground.

Although it wasn't quite dark yet, the fire was still spectacular, drawing a few people from around the place to come and have a look. There were a couple of cars parked on the side of the road, faces pushed against the windows, watching in awe. Tess smiled. She used to do the same thing when she was little, sitting in Pop's ute watching from the comfort of the driver's seat.

As she was looking at the parked cars, she caught a glimpse of the McGregor house just up the road. Curiously, there were lights on in the house. There hadn't been anyone in the McGregor house for years, except for a few holidayers every now and then. No-one willingly holidayed in Chesterfield unless they were visiting family, and even then, they'd normally stay at one of the motels in town.

"Tess!" She jerked her head around and saw Lonny waving madly at her. "Spot over," he yelled. Tess followed where he was pointing. An ember had fallen into the grass beside the festival block not far from where she was standing and had caught alight. She ran as fast as she could, pumping the handle on the spray pack as she went to build up pressure in the tank.

When she reached the spot over, she sprayed around the fire instead of directly onto it like she'd been taught, so she didn't flick up any more embers. Gary Evans had heard Lonny as well and ran over with his fire rake to pull away the grass to make a dirt break around it so it didn't spread. They managed to put it out without too much effort.

"Nearly," Gary said with a huff. He leant on his fire rake to catch his breath.

Tess looked back over to Lonny, who shook his head, but she thought she saw a smile on his face.

"Bet you're excited to be done with school," Gary said.

"I guess," Tess replied.

Gary nodded. "Jay couldn't wait to get to that big party down on the Gold Coast. Left the day after the formal. You kids heading down there?"

"I'm staying back to help out with the festival," Tess replied. "Lizzie and Will are away until the middle of the week but they're coming back for the festival too. Dad said if I didn't go to Schoolies he'd buy me a car next year, so you know, it was an easy decision."

"I'll bet," Gary said. "Have you heard from your folks yet?"

"They rang when they got into London, but it's been emails since then. The time zones are hard to work out," Tess said. Her dad wasn't coping well with the cold, but her mum was excited to be seeing snow for the first time as they toured around the UK.

"I hear ya," Gary said. "It's hard enough to work out when to ring Matty when he's on shift in WA. And that's only two hours difference. I think." He scratched his cheek. "Any plans for next year?"

"Uni, if I get in," Tess replied.

Gary scratched the orange stubble on his chin. "Back in my day, we finished school and went off to work the next morning. None of this partying stuff until we were twenty-one." He sniffed. "Unless you knew the barman at the local. Then you might get a few drinks before then. You kids don't know how lucky you've got it nowadays," he said. "Only waiting 'til eighteen to drink." He shook his head. "Of course, you only went to uni when you wanted to be a doctor or lawyer or something fancy like that. You need a bloody degree to turn on a TV these days."

"Spot over!" Lonny called again, saving Tess from the rest of Gary's lecture.

The block was a small one, so it wasn't long before the fire had burned itself out. Though the flames were gone, black cane trash still floated down from the sky as Gary and Tess headed back over to the ute. As she took off her spray pack, she glanced up at the McGregor house. The lights were still on, but she couldn't see any movement.

Pop tossed a fire rake into the back of the ute and opened the driver's side door. "You coming down the sheds with me?" he asked.

"I'll go up and help Gran out," Tess said. "Who's up at the McGregor's?"

Pop glanced across the cane paddock and shrugged. "Renters I suppose," he said and closed the door. Tess lifted the tailgate and clicked it shut. She banged on the side to let Pop know he could get going and headed back to the house. She'd have to ask Gran about the McGregor place to find out more.

Two

RUNNING IN THE COUNTRY was different from the city. In the city, depending on what time she got outside on a Sunday, Maddie Lambert would be negotiating other runners, bike riders, walkers, mothers with three-wheel all-terrain prams, and kids wobbling along on their bikes. Out here, the only thing she had to worry about was not getting an insect in her mouth. It had only happened once, and that was apparently because she'd been running at dusk. Or so Jo said. Maddie had decided to run in the middle of the day instead. Mornings had never been her strong point anyway, and she needed to run off the calories she'd eaten at the bakery earlier.

Indulging was something she hadn't been allowed to do for a long time, but as soon as she'd seen the size of those overfilled cream buns, she couldn't stop herself. Especially when she discovered it was real cream, and not the fake stuff most of the bakeries back home used. Her mouth watered at the thought of them. She'd definitely have to go back tomorrow to get another one. Of course, that would mean doing another run tomorrow afternoon. Or maybe she could just do an extra lap of the farm today.

As she ran along the track, kicking up red dust in her wake, she wondered how everyone else was coping since she'd walked out. Was she sorry to leave like she did? Sure, but no-one could say they hadn't seen it coming. At least Freya understood why she'd done it, and Andy couldn't resist the opportunity to take some time off and go surfing on the coast. Her father, on the other hand, wasn't so understanding.

They hadn't argued like that since Maddie was twelve and had wanted to go to the same public high school as the rest of her friends. He'd won that argument, but Maddie hadn't let him win this one. She hadn't spoken to him since she'd left, but Jo had called him to tell him they were safe.

As far as she knew, Jo hadn't let on where they were, which is what Maddie had wanted. If he found out, he'd be up in a flash trying to drag her back. She just couldn't deal with the way he was trying to micromanage every little part of her life anymore.

Her mother had started to get into the act as well, telling her what she should be wearing or how she should be getting her hair done. God, the look on her mother's face last week when

Maddie had appeared in cargo shorts and a t-shirt to go shoe shopping was priceless. Not having any make-up on was what had sent her mother over the edge. "You never know who might see you," her mother had said. "You have to go out in public as if you're going to be photographed. Do you have any idea what people would say if they saw you dressed like that?"

"How about 'there's a nice, down-to-earth-looking girl'?" Maddie had replied. Her mother turned up her nose and said, "You're not going looking like that." So, Maddie had stayed home, which annoyed her mother even more.

Without realising it, she'd increased her pace to almost a sprint. She slowed back to a jog and then stopped at the corner of the track, gulping in deep breaths of hot, fresh air. She pulled the ear buds from her ears, leaned on the fence post and stretched. No car fumes out here. Just wide open spaces and a lot of red dirt.

When Jo had suggested they come up here, Maddie was dubious because really, who had ever heard of Chesterfield? Maddie certainly hadn't, and she was glad she hadn't made any jokes about the place since Jo had revealed it was where she was born. Jo hadn't mentioned how she felt about it now, but Maddie figured that you always feel a bit nostalgic for the town you were born, even if you left when you were little, like Jo had.

And the house they were staying in was nice enough. Quaint, her mother would call it, but not in a good way. Nothing like their white concrete fortress in Mosman. The farm house felt comfortable, and lived in. Jo said she thought it was built in the 1920s, and the sag in the front veranda seemed to agree with that.

The walls had knocks and scrapes and dents in them, and it seemed to absorb sound. Unlike Maddie's place where you could hear someone coming down the stairs from the other end of the house. It used to freak her out when they'd first moved in a few years ago, the way it echoed every little sound when people were moving around in it. Then it would be deathly quiet at night.

The creaks in the farm house had kept her awake that first night too, but they felt different somehow. Jo had said the next morning that it was just the house settling as it cooled. It had creaked as they'd been talking about it that morning and Jo said it was expanding as it heated up. Almost like the house was a living, breathing thing. Maddie couldn't believe she didn't know that stuff. Basic science, Jo had said, which kind of explained it. Science had never been Maddie's strong point. She was more into the creative arts.

She finished stretching and looked back down the road she'd run on. It was a long way back, but she'd seen a side road somewhere that could be a shortcut back to the farm house.

She pushed the ear buds back into her ears and took off at a steady pace. The side track appeared just ahead, and the heavy guitar riff pumping through her ears and into her chest spurred her on, making her feel invincible. She turned the corner onto the unknown track, not caring if it was a shortcut and just happy to be away from the pressures of the last few months.

Three

TESS WAS RIDING ALONG the boundary line on the farm bike, heading out to where Pop, Lonny and Pete were finishing the harvesting, and all of a sudden, a streak of white shot out from the long grass in front of her. She clamped down on the brakes, locking up the wheels and sliding into the grass on Fitzy's side of the boundary. She stretched around to check behind her and gasped when she saw a girl lying, dazed, on the track. She dropped the bike and ran, getting to the girl as she was picking herself up, holding her head

"Bloody hell. I didn't see you. You alright?" Tess asked, crouching down to help the girl up. She was caked in red dirt, and no amount of her trying to dust it off was going to change the fact that her white tracksuit was ruined. She was definitely not from around here dressed like that.

"I think so," the girl said. She tried to stand but stumbled sideways. Tess threw out her arms to catch her before she fell back down. The girl winced. "I think I hurt my ankle."

Tess helped her over to the side of the track and lowered her down so she was sitting on the grass. A pool of red was slowly forming on her right knee. "Looks like you've got a graze as well," Tess said.

The girl pulled up the leg of her pants and prodded at her knee, sucking in a breath as little red droplets of blood oozed from the patch of raw skin. "Great. That's just fantastic." She blew out a breath and pushed a strand of white-blond hair behind her ears.

"It doesn't look too bad," Tess offered. "It's just a couple of layers of skin. Paw paw ointment will clear that up in no time."

The girl looked up, shading her face with her hand. "A paw paw will fix my graze?"

Tess shook her head. "The ointment, not the fruit. I have no idea if it's made from actual paw paws, but that's what it's called. And yes, it will fix your graze. Slather it on, cover it up and in a day or so, no more scab."

"You're talking from experience," the girl replied, pulling her pants leg back down.

Tess grinned. "When you ride bikes and spend your holidays on a farm, you get a lot of grazes."

The girl smiled back. "You're from around here then?"

"I live in town. I stay out here with my grandparents on the holidays."

The girl nodded. There was an awkward silence, so Tess asked, "What are you doing out here?"

"I'm staying in the house up the road for a few weeks."

"Holidays?"

"Sort of."

It had been ages since the last time any of the holidayers staying at the McGregor's had been Tess's age. It would be fun having someone to hang out with while Lizzie and Will were away. "Well, since we'll be neighbours for a few weeks, I guess we should introduce ourselves." She stuck out her hand. "I'm Tess."

The girl dusted her hand off on her pants, took Tess's hand, gave it a shake and said, "Maddie."

"Why are you running in a tracksuit in the middle of the day?" Tess asked, sitting down beside Maddie.

"It burns more calories," Maddie replied.

Burning calories had never been something Tess had ever really thought about. "If you're going to run during the day, you should probably stick to Fitzy's farm. He doesn't work the side closest to the McGregor house anymore."

"So no run-ins with reckless motorbike riders on that side?"

Her nose crinkled when she smiled, Tess noticed. "Highly unlikely," Tess replied. "Though in this weather, you should probably watch out for snakes."

"Really?" Maddie shifted forward a little, away from the long grass.

"It's summer," Tess shrugged. "They'll be out everywhere, and Fitzy's is so overgrown, I wouldn't be surprised if he has a whole country full of them over there."

"I'll keep an eye out for them," Maddie said.

Tess checked her watch and sucked in a breath through her teeth. "Bugger. I'm late."

"What for?"

"I'm just dropping off some lunch to my Pop."

"You should get going," Maddie said. "I don't want to get you into trouble."

Tess hesitated. "I can't leave you out here like this. Gran would kill me." She thought about Maddie's possible sprained ankle. It was a long walk back to the McGregor house, even without a limp. Pop would just have to wait a bit longer. "I can take you back if you like," she offered.

"Are you sure?"

"Of course. It'll save you limping all that way on a sore ankle. I'll just have to drop off lunch first though, if that's okay."

"Sure," Maddie said. "I'd never turn down a free ride."

Tess stood and helped Maddie up. Maddie tried to brush off the red dirt from her tracksuit again. "God, is all the dirt around here this red?"

"Yeah" Tess said, helping Maddie over to the bike. "Can't get it out of anything once it gets in.

White probably wasn't the best choice to wear out here."

"I'll keep that in mind," Maddie replied.

Tess picked up the bike, kick started it and adjusted the soft cooler she'd strapped to the handle bars, hoping that the drinks hadn't been shaken up too much. She turned to Maddie and patted the seat behind her. "Hop on."

The seat dropped under the extra weight and Tess felt Maddie take hold of her shirt. "You might want to hang on a bit tighter," Tess said. "Don't want you hitting the dirt again."

Maddie's arm snaked around Tess's waist. In her hurry to get going, Tess let out the clutch too fast, causing the bike to jolt forward. Maddie squealed and squeezed Tess tighter. The last time Tess had doubled someone on the bike was when Will's bike had run out of fuel last summer. It occurred to her that Will holding her around the waist didn't feel as good as it did with Maddie.

·♥·♥·♥·♥·♥·

It was easy to spot where the men were harvesting thanks to the plume of red dust billowing out from behind the harvester and haul out truck. This was the last big block to be done before they made a start on the small blocks near the house, so the farm was almost entirely an ocean of red dirt, criss-crossed with grassy tracks and dirt roads and cane trash waiting to be raked into rows. Further out past the watery heat mirages were the green tops of new sugar cane growth, and on a clear day, you could see right across three farms and almost to the edge of town.

As they crested a hill, Tess slowed and pointed out the harvester and haul out truck following beside it to Maddie. Pop's ute was parked at the end of the block. He'd probably be sitting in the cab waiting. At least Tess had a good excuse for why she was late.

She pulled the bike up at the back of the ute and killed the engine. Maddie stepped off and Tess unstrapped the cooler. The passenger-side door opened and Pop stepped out. "Man's not a camel," he said, his leathery face crinkling up with his smile.

"Sorry. Almost had an accident," Tess said, handing the cooler to Pop.

Pop looked from Tess to Maddie and Tess explained, "I almost ran her over."

"On purpose?" Pop asked.

Tess knew he was teasing, so instead of taking the bait she said, "Pop, this is Maddie. She's staying in the McGregor house."

"I know," Pop said. "How are you finding it? Got everything you need?" He dug into the cooler and pulled out a can of soft drink. He rolled it across his forehead and then popped the top and had a long drink.

"It's good. Thanks," Maddie replied.

Pop nodded.

"Are you going to be finished in time to start setting up?" Tess asked.

Pop glanced toward the harvester, scratched the back of his head and said, "We should be, but it doesn't matter. Lonny and Pete will just come back and finish it off tomorrow if they have to. There's still plenty of time to set up. Don't worry."

The one thing Tess looked forward to all year was spending the week leading up to the Crush Festival with Gran and Pop, helping them with the set up and then helping out during the festival. "Weather looks good this weekend for the burn."

"How do you know that?" Pop asked. He popped the lid on a plastic container and dug out a biscuit.

"I have a weather app on my phone."

Pop shook his head. He still used the weather service bulletins from the Rural Fire Service. They said the same thing, but Tess's way was more up-to-date. She'd never tell him that though.

"Are you having a bonfire or something?" Maddie asked.

"We've got the Crush Festival on," Tess said. "The grand finale is burning the small block of cane near the house."

"Sounds interesting."

"Don't get too excited," Pop said. "We only got a couple hundred people last year." He sighed. "Crowds have been getting smaller every year."

"Will, Lizzie and I are giving up Schoolies to be here this year," Tess said. "We'll get people in. We always do."

"We'll see," Pop said. "I should have some lunch so I can give Lonny his break."

"I'll see you back at the house," Tess said, climbing onto the bike and starting it up. Maddie slid on behind her, wrapping both arms around Tess this time. Tess waved to Pop and then headed off up to the McGregor house.

When they pulled up out front of the McGregor house, a woman rushed out onto the veranda and stopped dead on the top of the steps. "Maddie?" she said. She didn't look happy.

"Everything's fine. I'll be up in a minute."

The woman glared at Tess and then turned and walked back inside.

"I hope I didn't upset your mum," Tess said.

"She's not my mum, and no, if anyone's upset her, it's me."

"Are you going to be okay? Getting up the stairs I mean."

"I can manage. And I'll get some of that ointment you told me about, for my knee. Thanks for dropping me back."

"No problem. See that place over there?" Tess pointed to the old stucco farm house a hundred or so metres up on the other side of the road.

Maddie shielded her eyes with her hand and said, "Yeah."

"That's my grandparents' farm. I'm staying up there for the next few weeks if you need anything."

Maddie smiled and said, "Thanks. I'll be fine."

Tess started the bike and said, "I guess I'll catch you later then."

"I guess so."

As she rode back to the house, Tess mentally kicked herself for not giving Maddie her phone number. Just in case she needed anything.

Four

"WHAT HAVE YOU DONE this time?" Jo took Maddie's arm and draped it over her shoulder, leading her into the kitchen.

"You say that like I injure myself all the time," Maddie said, limping beside Jo.

"Tripping down the steps of a caravan," Jo said. "Running into a glass door at a motel. Catching your toe on the corner of a coffee table. And that's just in the last month. Should I go on?"

"No," Maddie replied. She didn't need to hear about slamming her finger in the limousine door last week or banging her head on the bottom of her desk a couple of days ago.

"So? What happened?" Jo asked again.

"I was running," Maddie said.

Jo didn't look like she believed it but she said, "Come and sit down and I'll have a look."

"I'm fine," Maddie said, trying not to wince as she hobbled along the hallway using Jo as support. She dropped down onto a chair at the table and Jo sat down across from her. She lifted Maddie's leg onto her lap and examined her ankle.

"There's a little bit of swelling," she said, turning it carefully in her hands. She moved Maddie's foot sideways, making Maddie wince. "It doesn't look like it's enough to be broken though." She stood up, pushed her chair closer to Maddie and placed her foot down. She took some ice from the freezer, wrapped it in a tea towel and wet it under the tap. "Hold," she said, placing it on Maddie's ankle.

Maddie did as she was told, and Jo sat down on the other side of the table. She folded her arms across her chest and though Maddie wasn't looking at her, she could feel Jo's glare.

This was one of Jo's tactics. Sit and stare and not say anything until Maddie got too uncomfortable and just had to say something. Maddie didn't give in this time though, because she was too focused on her sore ankle. She moved it a little and sucked in a breath. The cold got too much so she moved the ice pack to the other side of her ankle.

Finally, Jo uncrossed her arms and asked, "Who's the girl?"

"Her name is Tess and she lives up the road."

"And why was she bringing you back here on the back of a motorbike?"

"Because she's nice."

"That still doesn't explain what happened."

Maddie sighed. "I was running and not paying attention and I ran out in front of her. She almost ran over me but—"

Jo slapped her hand on the table. "Jesus, Maddie. You know I have to take you back in one piece, right?"

Maddie rolled her eyes. "It's just a sprain."

"We'll let a doctor decide that I think."

"I'm fine," Maddie said. "Really."

"You don't have a choice," Jo said.

"Fine," Maddie said. "But it'll have to be after my hair appointment."

Jo shook her head.

"What?" Maddie took the ice pack off and put it on the table. Jo raised her eyebrows and Maddie placed the ice pack back on her ankle.

"Don't you think that's going a bit too far?" Jo asked.

"Doing something I want with my hair instead of what someone else thinks I should do? Why is that a bad thing?" Maddie couldn't remember the last time she'd had a say over her 'look'.

"You won't be getting the same type of service up here. Not like the salons in Sydney."

It was Maddie's turn to shake her head. "I don't care. This," she said, holding out a handful of her bleached-blond hair, "was not my choice. I never wanted to be blond. But oh no, image is everything, isn't it? And no-one pays attention to the girl with mousy-brown hair." That's what her own mother had said to her just over a year ago. It had been easier then to just let her mother have her own way, but she wasn't going to let either of her parents run her life any more.

Jo held her hands up in surrender and said, "Alright, alright. You're talking to someone who gets a twenty dollar haircut from whoever can fit her in. Just understand that when your father goes ballistic, I'm not stepping in this time to help you out."

"Fine," Maddie shrugged.

"Speaking of your father, he called again."

"And?" He'd called Maddie's phone too and left messages that she'd deleted without even listening to. She didn't need to hear him telling her what he thought she should be doing anymore.

"And, you should talk to him, Maddie. He's worried."

Maddie snorted.

"Regardless of what you think of him, he's still your father, and he just wants what's best for you."

"What's best for him, you mean."

Jo didn't counter that point and instead changed tack. "Freya has left a heap of messages too. If you just do one thing, can you please call her? She doesn't deserve to be left in the dark."

"She knows what's going on," Maddie said, though she knew that wasn't exactly true. All Freya knew was that Maddie had had a massive fight with her father. She had no idea what it was about, and if she told Freya the truth, she'd be devastated. Besides, Maddie hadn't decided what she wanted to do yet, so it wasn't fair for her to dump everything on Freya without a solution. And there was Andy to think about too, though he'd probably just shrug and get back to his surfing.

"I'll call her later," Maddie said. Though it was to pacify Jo, she did think Freya deserved to at least know she was okay.

"Good," Jo replied, apparently satisfied. She pushed away from the table and walked over to the fridge and started pulling food out. "I thought we'd do hot dogs for lunch."

Maddie smiled. "Really? I thought they were full of crap?"

Jo laughed. "You're on holidays, so a little bit of bad food won't hurt."

Maddie decided against telling Jo about the cream bun from this morning. That would count as her bad food allowance for the day, so hot dogs would be off the lunch menu. Thinking about lunch, she thought about what Tess had been talking about with her Pop earlier. "Hey," she said. "What do you know about the Crush Festival?"

"Why do you ask?"

"Tess mentioned something about it."

"I didn't know it was still going," Jo said.

"What do you mean?"

"The Copeland's use to burn the last block of cane for the district and I think they just put on a bit of a party for whoever wanted to come."

"Oh," Maddie said. "So it's not very exciting then?" She was mildly disappointed. Though Tess's Pop had said it wasn't much at all, Tess seemed to be excited by it.

"It was when I was little I suppose, but I left when I was five or six so I don't remember too much about it." Jo turned and leaned against the bench. "I haven't been back in a long time, Maddie, so it could've changed since then. Did Tess say when it's on?"

"Next weekend."

"We can go if you like."

Maddie nodded.

"But," Jo said, pointing at Maddie with the cheese grater, "only if you stay injury free."

"Deal," Maddie replied.

Jo smiled and resumed making lunch.

Five

AFTER DINNER THAT NIGHT, Tess was in the kitchen helping with the dessert when Gran said, "Pop tells me you've met our new neighbours."

Tess stopped pouring custard into the serving jug and asked, "What did Pop say?"

"That you almost ran her over on the bike." She jabbed at Tess with a serving spoon. "You know I don't like you roaring around the farm on that thing. It's not safe."

"I wasn't going fast, and she was the one who ran out in front of me anyway."

"Well I'm just glad you didn't hurt the poor girl," Gran said, pouring chocolate sauce over the puddings.

"Actually," Tess said, "she kind of might have sprained her ankle. And got a graze on her knee. And her white tracksuit is ruined."

Gran clicked her tongue. "Has she got ointment?"

Tess shrugged. "I told her about it."

"You should take some over to her. And some washing powder. They're not from around here, so I doubt they'll have anything that can get red dirt out." Gran bent down and pulled a Tupperware container from the cupboard. She spooned in some chocolate pudding, poured over some custard and said, "And take this. As an apology for almost killing the poor girl."

"I didn't almost kill her."

Gran glared at Tess and Tess put her hands up in surrender. "Okay. I'll take it over and apologise." She didn't need to be told twice.

Gran nodded at the dessert plates and said, "Help me take these out."

Tess took two plates as well as the custard jug and followed Gran into the dining room where Pop, Lonny and Pete were talking.

Pete nodded his thanks when Tess handed him his dessert. Lonny, as usual didn't have any. He was skinny as a rake and would eat as much roast meat and vegetables as he could fit in but Tess had never seen him eat dessert. In fact, Tess thought, Gran's Sunday roast was most probably the main reason Lonny and Pete stayed out late to finish the harvesting. If they'd had to come back tomorrow, celebratory dinner would have been made by her, and the only thing she knew how to cook was spaghetti.

Tess poured custard over her pudding and settled into the conversation.

"Mary's got another treatment to go," Lonny said. "Then we have to just wait and see."

"Is she getting new ones?" Pete asked.

"New ones what?" Tess asked.

"New boobs," Lonny said.

"Oh," Tess said. She must have looked confused because Gran said, "Mary opted for a double mastectomy, just in case."

"Oh," Tess replied. She knew Lonny's wife had been diagnosed with cancer but didn't know the extent of it. "I didn't know it was that bad."

"It's not," Lonny said. "She just wanted to make sure, that's all."

"You didn't answer the question," Pete said.

"Mary said once she's over everything and has the all clear, she's going to get a new set that would remind me of when she was in her twenties," Lonny said.

Tess almost spit out her pudding. Gran said, "I'm glad Mary's doing well Lonny, but I don't think breasts are appropriate dinner table conversation."

"Sorry," Lonny said. He turned to Pop. "Mary says you're still waiting on the cheque."

"Barry's supposed to drop it off this week," Pop replied.

"Did they give you what you wanted?" Lonny asked.

"Half," Pop said.

Pete shook his head. "Bloody council."

"Language," Gran said and Pete apologised. There were two rules at her table; no singlets and no swearing.

"They're not helping with the advertising either from what I've heard," Pop said.

"Idiots," Pete said. "Montgomery's probably siphoning of money for his campaign next year. Corrupt bast—" He stopped mid-sentence. "Sorry. Corrupt so-and-so," he said instead.

"It's not going to matter though, right?" Tess asked. "I mean, we still get a piece in the paper. Lizzie's dad puts something in every year for free, so that's something isn't it?"

"We can't just keep relying on the locals to come, Tess," Pop said. He tipped his bowl up to scrape out the last of his pudding. "People around here are all still suffering from the drought. They haven't got money to spend. The council was supposed to get us some advertising on the radio this year but I doubt that's gotten any further than a brain fart."

"Jack!" Gran said, and Tess had to stifle a giggle.

"Idiots," Pete said again, this time shaking his head to emphasise the point.

Pop sighed. "We're missing a lot of stallholders this year too. No-one seems to be interested anymore."

"Will and Lizzie and I will talk to everyone we know. We'll get through this year and then next year we'll—"

"There might not be a next year," Pop said, pushing himself away from the table and standing up. "I'll wash up," he said to Gran and walked into the kitchen.

"But—"

"Tess," Gran warned. When Tess looked at her she just shook her head.

Tess couldn't believe Pop was thinking about not having the festival anymore. Stupid council. We're just going to have to work out a way to make heaps of people come this year, she thought. If they made more money from it, they wouldn't have to rely on the council for grant money next year, and the council couldn't have a say in it. She'd talk to Lizzie and Will when they got back to see if they could come up with some ideas to take the pressure off of Pop.

"You should take that stuff over to Maddie before it gets too late," Gran said. She took Tess's empty bowl and placed it on top of hers. "I'll clean up."

"We should probably get going too," Lonny said, helping Gran stack the plates.

Tess pushed away from the table. Maybe a visit with Maddie might pick her up a bit.

Six

TESS WASN't exactly sure why, but she was feeling nervous walking up the stairs of the McGregor house. She couldn't decide whether it was the thought of seeing Maddie again that was making her feel like that, or the thought that the woman who Maddie said wasn't her mum didn't like her for some reason. She knocked on the screen door and stepped back. The woman she'd seen earlier that afternoon answered the door. "Yes?"

"Hi. I'm Tess," Tess said, trying not to sound nervous. "I brought some stuff to give to Maddie. If that's okay." She held out the containers in her hands.

The woman narrowed her eyes and for a moment, Tess thought she might not let her in. Eventually, she stepped aside, held the door open for Tess and said, "Maddie's in the lounge room."

"Thanks," Tess said and stepped inside. It had been a few years since Tess had been at the

McGregor's, but she remembered her way around. She walked straight down the hall past the front two bedrooms and took the third door on the right, where she found Maddie laying on the lounge in a t-shirt and shorts, her left leg resting on a pile of cushions. She sat up when she saw Tess.

"Hey, Tess."

"I just came to see how you were doing," Tess said.

"I'm good," Maddie replied. "My ankle's a bit swollen, but otherwise I'm okay."

"What about your graze?"

Maddie's eyes widened and she said, "Hurt like hell when I had a shower but it's not too bad now. I just have to stop bending my knee so much so it stops weeping."

Tess nodded. "I brought some paw paw ointment over for it. Gran didn't know if you'd have any." Tess offered it to Maddie, who took it and peered at the container.

"What else have you got there?" Maddie asked, stretching up to see.

"Oh, Gran made me bring some washing powder for your clothes. She makes some special blend that gets the red dirt out." Maddie took the container of powder, gave it a shake and placed it on the floor.

Tess continued, "And there's some chocolate pudding as well. I guess she was hoping it would be a good apology for me almost running you over today."

Maddie smiled and said, "So she made you come over?"

"Yeah, I mean, I was happy to come over. I was going to anyway, to see how you were, but she made me bring all this stuff."

"Uhuh," Maddie said. "Chocolate pudding?"

"Yeah. It's the best you've ever tasted," Tess said, handing Maddie the last container.

Maddie popped open the lid and breathed in. "It smells amazing."

"I could get you a spoon, if you want to try it?" Tess asked. Maddie grinned and nodded, and Tess headed out into the hallway and down to the kitchen at the back, where she found the woman who wasn't Maddie's mum sitting at the table tapping away at a laptop. She looked up when Tess entered. "I'm just after a spoon," Tess said.

The woman pointed to some drawers and Tess muttered a thanks. She could feel the woman's gaze on her as she left.

Tess handed Maddie the spoon and Maddie patted the lounge beside her. "Sit here," she said. Tess eased down beside the pile of cushions at the far end of the lounge so she didn't accidentally bump Maddie's foot.

"Are you in witness protection or something?" Tess whispered.

Maddie laughed. "Sometimes it feels like it." She dug into the pudding and sighed as she ate a spoonful. "Oh. My. God. That is so good."

"I know, right? Gran is the best baker in town. Wait til you taste her cupcakes. She's making a heap for the festival."

"What is the festival anyway?" Maddie asked around a mouthful of pudding. "I asked Jo but she said she couldn't remember much about it. Is it a music festival or something?"

Jo must be the woman in the kitchen, Tess thought. "It's to officially close the cane crushing season," Tess replied. "Gran and Pop have been having it for as long as I can remember."

"Every year?"

"Except for one year when the rains came a month early and flooded it out, but that was before I was born."

"What does it involve?"

"We have a few local bands come and play and sometimes one or two from Brisbane. There are food stalls and a jumping castle and rides, a side show alley, and Cow Pat Bingo. And when it's all over, the grand finale is burning the last block of cane."

Maddie ditched the spoon and ran her finger around the inside of the container. 'Fingers are not cutlery' Gran would have said if she'd seen Maddie do that.

Wait," Maddie said. "What's Cow Pat Bingo?"

"You mark out squares in a paddock," Tess explained. "People buy the numbers, and then wait for Bessie, she's the cow, to poo on one of them."

Maddie laughed. "Really? People bet on where a cow will poo?"

"Of course. I can't believe you've never heard of it before. I thought all school fetes had it."

"I was home schooled for the last part of high school." Apparently satisfied that she'd eaten every last bit of pudding and custard, Maddie snapped the lid back on the container and handed it to Tess.

Tess wondered what it would've been like, not having to go to school every day like everyone else and just do it at home. She couldn't imagine not seeing Will and Lizzie every day at school. "Well, you have to come to the festival on the weekend. You'll love it."

"I will." Maddie smiled.

"Or you could come and help set up. If you're not doing anything else."

Maddie's eyes lit up. "Yeah. I think I might."

"You shouldn't be going anywhere on that ankle." The woman who Tess assumed was Jo, stood in the doorway, her arms crossed.

Maddie glanced up at her and then back at Tess. "I'll see what the doctor says. Can I let you know?"

Tess nodded. "Definitely see how you feel. Don't want you to hurt your ankle again."

"Can you give me your phone number?" Maddie asked. "So I can text you in the morning?"

"Okay." Tess wished that she found it so easy to ask girls for their phone numbers.

Maddie turned to Jo. "Can you get me my phone from my room? Please?"

Jo sighed and walked away. Tess got the distinct feeling she wanted Tess to be gone.

Tess leaned toward Maddie and said, "She's not going to shoot me, is she? I feel like she's just waiting for the right time to pop me off."

Maddie laughed. "Jo's harmless. She's just overprotective."

"So is she your, um, sister? Or something?"

Before Maddie could answer, Jo had returned with Maddie's phone. Maddie entered Tess's number into her phone and then gave Tess her number. "Just so you know it's not some random stalker texting you," she said.

"Thanks."

"It's late," Jo said. She raised her eyebrows.

Tess guessed that was her cue so she stood up, shoved her phone into her shorts pocket and said, "I should get going. I have to work tomorrow morning anyway." She glanced over at Jo, who seemed to be the only one not smiling. She looked back to Maddie and said, "I guess I might see you tomorrow."

"I hope so," Maddie said.

Tess squeezed past Jo, who didn't move from her spot in the doorway and headed to the front door. As she closed the door behind her, she could hear Jo and Maddie talking in raised voices. She hoped she hadn't gotten Maddie in trouble, because she thought she'd really like to see her again tomorrow.

Later that night, Tess was lying in bed reading when her phone buzzed. Her heart skipped a beat at the thought that it might be Maddie. When she picked up her phone and saw that it wasn't her heart dropped a little. It was a text from her best friend Lizzie, who was in Brisbane to see a concert.

Met the band OMG so cool! Indiana Rose MIA Maybe sick Hope she's better for the concert xx

Tess text back **Have fun xx**

Seven

JO HAD SOMEHOW MANAGED to sweet talk a receptionist into getting Maddie in to see the doctor early on Monday morning before any other patients arrived and it turned out that she did just have a sprain. A day or two on crutches and she should be fine according to the doctor. All that might change though when Jo saw what Maddie had done with her hair. She'd probably freak out about her getting it cut rather than just the colour change they'd discussed, but Maddie didn't care. The hairdresser had thought Maddie had been through a particularly bad breakup because she wanted such a drastic change, and Maddie had let her believe it. It was kind of true. Maddie also thought she'd felt sorry for her being on crutches, because when she'd gone to pay, the hairdresser had told her the foils were on the house. Regardless of what Jo thought, Maddie felt a lot less like the girl everyone thought they knew and a lot more like she used to be.

Since she had half an hour to kill before she had to meet Jo at the post office, Maddie decided to call into the bakery to see if they had any more of those delicious and dangerous cream buns she'd discovered the day before.

The bell on the door tinkled Maddie's arrival as she opened it and the smell of fresh bread and sugar engulfed her as she pushed her way in. She was struggling to hold the door open with her shoulder as she manoeuvred her crutches up the single step into the shop when all of a sudden, the door was pulled back. Grateful for the help, Maddie muttered a thanks and when she looked up, she was surprised to see it was Tess. "Hi," Maddie said.

Tess took a moment to recognise her and when she did, she grinned broadly and replied, "Hey, Maddie. I like your hair."

"Thanks," Maddie replied, smiling in return.

"Short really suits you," Tess said. "What made you change it?"

Maddie followed Tess over to the counter. "I just felt like something different and decided to go back to my natural colour."

Tess nodded and said, "I've never been anything other than my natural colour."

"If I had your colour, I don't think I'd change it either," Maddie said. Tess had a nice shade of dark blond with what Maddie assumed were natural sun-bleached streaks. Probably from being outside a lot, judging from the limited amount Maddie knew about her.

Tess touched her hair and made a face. "Really?"

Maddie shrugged. "Yeah. That was the look I thought I was getting when I went blond but it didn't turn out that way."

"Well, not that I didn't like it before, but I prefer the new look."

"Thanks." The fact that someone liked her new look might make Maddie feel better when Jo said she hated it. She shifted her weight forward to get a better look at the display cabinet. Before she could catch herself, the left crutch slipped out from under her arm on the tiles and she stumbled sideways.

Tess rushed from behind the counter and caught her. Again. "Careful," Tess said, picking up the fallen crutch and handing it to Maddie.

"Thanks. I'm still getting used to them," Maddie replied.

"They take a bit of getting used to but you'll be right. Just stay away from stairs."

"I'll keep that in mind."

"No plaster," Tess said. "No break?"

"Just a sprain. The doctor said to stay off it for a few days and I should be okay."

Tess nodded. The way she looked at Maddie, a small smile on her lips, made Maddie's stomach flutter. Maddie looked away and made a point of scanning the display cabinet.

Tess walked back around behind the counter and asked, "What can I get you?"

"Do you have any of those cream buns?" Maddie asked. She couldn't see any in the cabinet.

"Sorry. Just sold the last one. The next lot won't be ready for a while. I'm the only one here until Mrs Brannigan gets back."

"Oh."

"What about a cream donut? Same thing except more sugar," Tess suggested.

"Like I need more sugar," Maddie replied, trying to decide if there was anything else she felt like. She hadn't thought past the cream bun.

"Like you don't," Tess said.

Maddie looked up. "What makes you say that?"

Tess shrugged. "You just don't look like you eat much sugar at all."

Maddie cocked her head.

"I mean, you just look too fit to eat too much junk food," Tess said.

Was Tess flirting? Maddie couldn't be sure. It had been a while since she'd been flirted with, but the thought that Tess might be flirting made her arms tingle. Or it could just be the loss of blood flow from leaning on her crutches. "I eat junk food," Maddie countered. "I'm just not supposed to eat it all the time."

"You're not one of those girls who are always on a diet?" Tess asked.

"You don't diet?" Maddie asked.

"My diet consists of anything I feel like eating," Tess said.

Maddie felt a little defensive and replied, "Well, some of us just try to eat well. Most of the time anyway."

"Except for cream buns," Tess said, raising an eyebrow.

Maddie relaxed. "Anything sweet really, but cream buns are my kryptonite."

"You probably shouldn't say that too loud," Tess whispered from behind her hand, looking around the shop.

Maddie leaned in and whispered back, "Why not?"

"Because once someone knows your weakness, it's easy for them to take advantage." Tess smiled.

Definitely flirting, Maddie thought. Two can play at that game. "Too bad you've got none left then," Maddie replied.

Tess laughed. Before Maddie could say anything else, the doorbell tinkled.

"Sorry I took so long, Tess," said the woman who entered. She was wearing an oversized straw hat and was carrying an armful of bags. Tess hurried over to help her and the woman swept her hat off her head, letting loose a mop of grey curls, and strode around behind the counter. "Oh," she said, noticing Maddie for the first time. "Hello."

"Mrs Brannigan, this is Maddie," Tess said, placing the bags on the back counter. "She's staying up at the McGregor's."

"Hi," Maddie said.

"Maddie's a fan of your cream buns," Tess said.

"Is that so?"

Maddie nodded.

"We should have some more out shortly," Mrs Brannigan said. She turned to Tess. "I'll just drop this stuff in the office and be out so you can get back to the buns. Nice to meet you, Maddie." She rushed into the back and out of sight.

"Do you want to wait?" Tess asked. "They shouldn't be too long."

Maddie checked her watch. "It's okay. I have to meet Jo anyway." She turned to leave and Tess walked around the counter and held the door open for her. Maddie safely negotiated the one step down onto the footpath and steadied herself.

"We'll be starting the festival preparations tomorrow," Tess said, leaning on the door. "If you're up for it, you're welcome to come over."

"I haven't got any plans," Maddie replied. "But I should probably check with Jo."

"Okay," Tess said. "See you later."

"See you," Maddie smiled. She turned and hobbled off in the direction of the post office. She was still struggling to get used to the crutches and had managed to make it a few metres without falling over when she stumbled.

"Do you want me to come with you?" Tess called. "Just in case you need me to catch you if you fall?"

Maddie stopped and turned and poked out her tongue. Tess waved and went back inside. Maddie couldn't help but smile.

Eight

THAT AFTERNOON, TESS WAS raking the leaves from under the mango tree in the Big Yard, wondering how she could have embarrassed herself so badly in front of Maddie that morning. Telling her she's fit? God, how cliché. She thought Maddie was pretty good looking, especially with her new short hair style, but it wasn't something you just came out and told a girl was it? Especially not when you'd just met them.

Then again, Tess was pretty sure Maddie was flirting with her with the whole cream bun thing. She wondered if she liked cupcakes. She said she had a sweet tooth.

Tess's thoughts were interrupted by someone calling her name. She looked up to see Will striding across the yard.

"Got you doing the easy stuff," Will said, wrapping Tess in a hug.

"The boring stuff," Tess said, leaning the rake against the wheelbarrow. "I didn't think you were going to be here until Thursday."

Will shrugged. "They cancelled my interview."

"Wow. Really?" Will had applied for an entry level conservation job on the Coast. He'd wanted to be a ranger ever since he'd met Ranger Stacey in third grade. Tess thought he still secretly crushed on her. "What happened?"

"They said they're not filling it yet."

"Can they do that?"

"I guess so. Anyway, it doesn't matter. I'll get to interview for it later hopefully. Besides, it means I get a few extra days at home with you and Lizzie." He was smiling, but Tess could tell he was disappointed. "Hey, speaking of Lizzie, did you hear the concert's been cancelled?" he asked.

Tess hadn't heard from Lizzie since her text last night. "No. What happened?"

"No idea," Will said. "Lizzie's crushed. She called me just before and had a bit of a rant about it."

"I can imagine. She's been waiting all year for it. Are they rescheduling?"

"No idea. I'm sure Lizzie will tell us all about it when she gets home."

Tess nodded.

"How's the prep going?" Will asked.

Tess shrugged. "Just cleaning up at the moment. Pop hasn't given me anything else to do yet, but Gran's started the baking. I think she's doing the coconut ice this morning and then cupcakes this afternoon."

"I might go see if she wants me to taste test for her," Will said.

"Ha! Good luck with that," Tess laughed.

"Hey, I saw a car in the drive way at McGregor's. Is someone staying there?" Will asked.

"Yeah. They've been there a couple of days I think."

"Renters?"

"Holidayers. There's a girl, our age, called Maddie. And a woman who isn't her mother called Jo."

"Sounds curious. I wonder what their story is."

"No idea," Tess replied. "But Maddie seems alright."

"Mm hhm," Will said.

"I've run into her a couple of times in the last few days," Tess said. "Literally."

"What do you mean?"

"She ran out in front of me yesterday when I was on my way up the farm. I almost hit her on the bike."

"You didn't hurt her did you?" Will asked.

"She's okay," Tess said. "Just a sprained ankle and a bit of a graze."

Will shook his head. "You know there are better ways to meet girls, don't you?"

"You should've seen her this morning trying to work out how to use the crutches. She almost fell over in the shop. It was just lucky I was there to catch her."

"Really?"

"Yeah," Tess said, laughing. "It was so funny."

Will narrowed his eyes. Tess said, "What?"

Will shook his head. "Nothing. Is Pop around?"

"In the tractor shed I think."

"Cool. I'll go and see if he needs a hand with anything." He turned to leave and then turned back and said, "Just so you know, I've entered the comp tonight."

Tess rolled her eyes. "Again? Don't you want to give someone else a chance to win best belly flop?"

"No way. That free ice cream is all mine." Will rubbed his hands together. "You're coming to watch me win, right?"

"Do I have a choice?"

"No."

"Fine."

"Great. It's a date. You should ask Maddie if she wants to come."

Before Tess could answer, he wandered off toward the old tractor shed, hands shoved into his pockets, his thongs flipping up against the bottom of his feet. Pop would make him change into joggers before he'd let him start helping with anything. In fact, Will would be lucky if Pop even let him into the shed with thongs on.

As Tess picked up the rake to continue clearing up the leaves, her phone buzzed in her pocket. She dug it out and swiped the screen. She smiled when she saw it was a text from Maddie.

Thanks for dropping the cream bun off.

Tess text back No worries Hope it was worth the wait.

Sure was :)

Tess thought about what Will said. She sent Belly flop comp at the pool tonight Tragic but funny You're welcome to come.

There was a bit of a wait and then Maddie replied Sure Meet you there What time?

6?

It's a date :)

Tess wondered what she should reply and before she could decide, her phone buzzed with another text.

This one was from Lizzie. My life sux Concert cancelled :(Heading home See you tomorrow.

Tess replied I'll be here

Might need comfort food

Gran's big breakfast?

Perfect Your gran is awesome :)

I know See you tomorrow

Tess shoved her phone back into her pocket. She smiled at the thought of seeing Maddie again and getting to see Lizzie tomorrow and continued raking.

Nine

IT WAS SO HOT that being in the pool was a welcome relief. The coolness of the water also seemed to be taking the edge off the pain in Maddie's ankle. The swelling had gone down but the bruising had come out so it looked worse than it actually was. Plus, Jo had caught her hobbling around the house without her crutches, which was probably a stupid idea, but it was so hard to move around the furniture without bumping into things or knocking things over. Jo was this close to not letting Maddie go out, but in the end, she'd been invited to meet up with some of her family at the pub just up the road from the pool, so they came to a compromise. Since Jo and her family in Chesterfield didn't exactly get on the best, Maddie could stay at the pool for as long as Jo managed to stay at the pub.

"I can't believe your parents didn't take you to Europe with them," Maddie said.

"I wanted to stay," Tess said.

"You willingly chose summer in Chesterfield over winter in Europe?" Maddie asked.

Tess shrugged. "There's nothing wrong with Chesterfield," she said.

"No, I didn't mean it like that," Maddie said. She hadn't meant to offend Tess. "I just mean that I thought it would've been a no-brainer."

"You would've gone to Europe?" Tess asked.

"If my parents were paying? Sure," Maddie nodded.

"Yeah, well, it took mum and dad five years to save up and if I'd gone, they wouldn't have been able to go to all the places they're going to."

"So you gave up a white Christmas just so your parents could have one?"

"Sure," Tess shrugged. "Why not? Anyway, I love summer. Don't you?"

Maddie drooped lower into the water and said, "I like the less extreme seasons a lot better. You don't feel like you're going to melt."

"That's why swimming was invented."

Maddie smiled. She brought her knees up to her chest and prodded at her graze.

"I'm glad your knee's clearing up okay," Tess said, waving her hands under the water causing little ripples on the surface.

"That paw paw ointment worked a treat," Maddie replied.

"Told you," Tess said.

Maddie had been a bit dubious about the ointment but when Jo had agreed on its apparent magical graze-healing properties, Maddie figured it couldn't hurt to try it out. "Pity it doesn't work on sprained ankles," she said.

Tess laughed and replied, "There's only so much a paw paw can do."

Maddie splashed Tess, and Tess splashed her back.

"Hey, watch it," Will said, as he slipped into the water. Tess and Maddie both splashed him and he laughed. "All registered," he said. "They said they're starting in about ten minutes. And you're straight after me, Maddie. Lucky last."

"Wait a minute," Tess said. "You registered?"

"Uhuh," Maddie nodded.

"How are you going to get up onto the diving board with your ankle?"

"I'll be fine," Maddie said. "But I might need someone to stand up there with me, just to steady me before I dive."

She smiled sweetly at Tess, who shook her head. "Not me. No way."

"Come on, Tess. Help an invalid out," Will said.

"Yeah, Tess, help an invalid out," Maddie said. "I'll share my ice cream with you when I win."

"My ice cream, you mean," Will said.

"Okay, Will will share his ice cream with you when I win," Maddie said, and Tess laughed.

"Wait a minute, that's not what I meant," Will said.

"Doesn't this fall into the 'doing something stupid' thing Jo was talking about?" Tess asked.

"What she doesn't know won't hurt her," Maddie replied.

Tess sighed. "Fine. I'll help you out."

Maddie turned to Will and asked, "Any tips on impressing the judges?"

"Well," Will said, "the bigger the splash, the more points they give you."

Maddie considered that and said, "Front or back?"

"Technically, you should hit with your stomach. It is a belly flop comp remember?"

"Right."

"Though last year, Travis Eastman came in second and he flipped over onto his back at the last minute and almost caused a tidal wave when he hit."

Maddie laughed.

"Of course," Will said, leaning in closer to Maddie. "Travis is about three times my size."

Tess slapped Will's arm and said, "Don't' be nasty."

Will shrugged. "It's the truth."

Tess stood up on the step she was sitting on and said, "If you two are going to talk tactics, I'm going to get a drink. Anyone else want one?"

Will shook his head, and Maddie said, "I'll have a water."

"I'll be back," Tess said. She stepped out of the pool and walked toward the kiosk.

As Maddie watched Tess leave, she noticed how dark Tess's legs looked against her light blue board shorts, and guessed her athletic build came from spending so much time outside and on a farm. It kind of sucked that Maddie had to exercise so much to keep her figure and yet Tess could just go about her business and still have a great body.

Will slid over beside her and said, "She's a good catch."

"What?"

"Tess. She's the best girl I know."

"Why are you telling me this?" Maddie asked.

Will shrugged. "You two just seem to be hitting it off. That's all."

"She's nice," Maddie said.

"Funny," Will said, smiling. "That's exactly what she said about you."

"You were talking about me?" Maddie asked. "When?"

"Today," Will said. "Couldn't shut her up."

"Really?" Maddie said.

Will grinned and nodded. Maddie looked over toward the kiosk. Tess turned around and waved. Maddie and Will waved back.

The PA crackled to life and asked everyone to clear the pool for the start of the Annual Chesterfield Community Pool Belly Flop Competition. Will helped Maddie out of the pool and back to their bags. Tess handed Maddie her water.

"Are you ready to see how it's done?" Will asked, stretching his back and arms.

"Bring it on," Maddie said.

·❤·❤·❤·❤·❤·

Maddie followed Tess up the stairs of the diving board. It was slow going having to try to hop up each rung, and it was hard for Maddie to stop herself from catching a glimpse of Tess'?s butt as she climbed up the stairs above her. When she reached the top, Maddie took the hand Tess offered to her, pulled herself up onto the platform and steadied herself. She wasn't afraid of heights but five metres was still higher than she'd thought.

"Ready?" Tess asked, and Maddie nodded.

Tess wrapped her arm around Maddie's waist to take the weight off her left foot and Maddie put her arm over Tess's shoulder. Slowly, they made their way to the end of the diving board. Maddie took a deep breath, smiled at Tess and said, "Let's do this."

"Wait a minute—" But before Tess could say anymore, Maddie had leapt off the diving board pulling Tess with her. Tess's screams were cut off as they hit the water together with a monumental splash. Maddie surfaced first and wiped the water off her face. She looked around for Tess, who surfaced behind her. When Maddie turned to apologise, Tess pushed a wall of water at Maddie with her hands. Maddie shook it off and laughed. They swam to the edge of the pool where Will helped them both out and handed them their towels.

"A tandem jump?" Will said. "I'm not sure that's legal."

"How was it?" Maddie asked, drying her hair off with her towel.

"It was pretty spectacular," Will said. He turned to Tess. "All this time I've known you, and I never knew you were a screamer."

Tess punched him on the arm.

"Scores are up," Will said. They all turned to the side of the pool where the judges sat on the tall lifesaver chairs. One by one, they revealed their scores. Two fours and a five. The announcement over the loud speaker confirmed Will's win. Will lifted his arms in the air in triumph and said, "Thank you, thank you. I'll be signing autographs at the gate later."

Then there was another announcement. "The judges have awarded an honourable mention to Maddie and Tess, for their spectacular tandem jump. Would the winners please come to the kiosk?"

"A chocolate Paddle Pop tastes so much better when you've won it," Will said, licking a drip from his finger.

"I second that," Maddie said, taking a bite from hers.

Tess crunched on her Cornetto cone. "I can't believe they only had two of them left," she said.

"I told you you could have it," Maddie said.

"It's fine. My Cornetto's just as good."

"Always the martyr," Will said.

Maddie's phone buzzed. "That's Jo," she said. "She'll be here in ten minutes." She finished off her ice cream and stood up, throwing her bag over her shoulder. "I should go and get changed. She won't let me in the car in wet clothes." Maddie pulled a crutch under each arm and as she turned to go, Tess said, "Do you need a hand?"

Maddie turned, her eyes narrowed and a smile playing on her lips. "I'll be fine, thanks," she said, and hobbled off.

When Maddie had disappeared into the change rooms, Will gave Tess a shove and said, "What was that?"

"What?" Tess asked, crunching the chocolate tip of her ice cream and scrunching up the empty wrapper.

Will mimicked Tess's voice and said, "Do you need a hand?"

"What are you talking about?" Tess asked.

"Think about it," Will said. "Imagine if it was me that had the hots for Maddie—"

"I don't have the hots for Maddie," Tess said.

Will raised his eyebrows but continued. "Imagine if I had the hots for some girl and she was going off to get changed and I asked her if she needed a hand."

Tess considered it for a moment and then burst out laughing. "I see what you mean," she said. She dropped her head onto the table. "Oh God. I must've sounded like an idiot."

Will patted her on the back. "It's okay. We all say stupid things when we're in love."

Tess whacked him on the leg and he laughed. If the number of times you made a fool of yourself in front of a person was dependent on how much you liked them, then it seemed like Tess really liked Maddie.

When Maddie returned from the change rooms, she said, "Jo's out in the car park, so I guess I'll see you later."

"Don't forget to ask Jo about tomorrow," Tess said.

"I'll let you know," Maddie replied.

"About what?" Will asked.

"The preparations for the festival," Tess said.

"Right," Will said. "There'll be plenty to do, even for an invalid."

Tess punched him on the arm. To Maddie, she said, "We'll be starting early though."

"How early?" Maddie asked.

"Lizzie and I will be there for breakfast," Will said. "You should come over then."

"Oh I wouldn't want to impose," Maddie said.

"You wouldn't be. Gran loves cooking for heaps of people," Will said. "Doesn't she Tess?"

"Yeah. Will turns up unannounced for food all the time," Tess said and laughed when Will slapped her playfully on the leg. "It'll be fine. I'll just let her know to expect you, that's all."

Maddie nodded. "Okay. Sure. I'll see you in the morning then."

As they watched Maddie leave, Will leaned in to Tess and said, "You're right you know."

"About what?"

"She is nice."

Tess smiled. "I know."

Later that night, Tess had just turned off her bedside lamp when she received a text. She reached over and picked up her phone from her bedside table. It was Maddie. Thanks for tonight I had heaps of fun

Me too

Looking forward to tomorrow Sure it's okay for me to come for breakfast?

Of course! Gran will be happy to have you Might be sorry when you ee what she's got you doing.

Like what?

You'll see tomorrow.

Sounds ominous.

You have no idea ;)

See you in the morning.

Tess smiled. Can't wait.

Night xx

Night.

Tess hesitated for a minute and then added 'xx' and pressed send.

She lay back on her pillow, closed her eyes and smiled. Just as she was drifting off, her phone buzzed again. She swiped the screen to see a message from Lizzie.

Who's the girl?

What girl?

In the pic.

Tess had no idea what Lizzie was talking about.

What pic?

The one Will sent.

There was a pause, and then a picture came through. Tess zoomed in to see it was a picture of her and Maddie standing on the diving board with their arms around each other. Will must have taken it before they dived into the pool. Her stomach fluttered seeing herself standing like that with Maddie. Of course, it was totally innocent, and Tess knew that. She was just helping Maddie steady herself on the diving board because of her ankle, but to anyone else watching, it could have looked like something more. She text Lizzie back.

That's Maddie She's staying at McGregor's.

And?

And what?

You look pretty close Anything I should know?

Tess thought about it for a moment and all the things she could say to Lizzie about the way she was starting to feel about Maddie. About how just the thought of seeing Maddie made her stomach flip. But she didn't really understand it herself yet, and besides, it was too hard to tell Lizzie over text message. So instead, she just said You'll get to meet her in the morning.

Lizzie replied Fine See u at breakfast x.

Can't wait to catch up x.

Ten

WHEN TESS WENT OUT for breakfast the next morning, Will, Lizzie and Maddie were all sitting around the table, tucking into bacon, eggs and toast.

"About time you got up," Will said, shovelling a forkful of bacon into his mouth.

"How long have you been here?" Tess asked, sitting down across from Maddie, who was sipping on what Tess assumed to be a cup of tea.

"Long enough for Will to be on his third helping," Lizzie said.

"I've got a big day ahead," Will said, mopping up the last of his eggs with a piece of toast.

"Sorry about the concert, Lizzie," Tess said. She poured herself some cornflakes, shook over some sugar, drowned it all in milk and dug in.

"Don't get her started," Will said, pushing his chair back and taking his breakfast dishes into the kitchen.

"I can't believe I drove all that way, just for the concert to be cancelled," Lizzie said.

"I told you not to get her started," Will called from the kitchen.

Tess ignored him and asked, "Do you know why?"

Lizzie shrugged. "One of the band members was sick or something apparently."

"Who were you going to see?" Maddie asked.

"Three's Company," Lizzie replied.

Maddie coughed.

"Are you alright?" Tess asked.

"Tea went down the wrong way," Maddie croaked, patting her chest with her hand.

"Are they rescheduling?" Tess asked Lizzie.

"I don't know. They just said the rest of their tour is cancelled until further notice."

"Wow. Sounds serious."

"Yeah. A couple of people on the fan site have said that they think they've broken up," Lizzie said, pulling the crusts from her toast and biting into the rest.

"Really?"

"Yeah, but who knows. I do know though, that no-one's seen Indiana Rose for a couple of weeks. She wasn't at the signing either." Lizzie leaned in and whispered, "There's even a rumour going around that she's gone to rehab."

Maddie coughed again. Tess glanced at her and Maddie was looking into her teacup as if there was something in there making her cough.

"I thought they were a clean band?" Tess asked, fishing the last of the cornflakes from her bowl and tipping it up to drain the last of the milk. Which she would never normally do except Gran wasn't there to chastise her.

"Publicity," Will said. He leaned on the door frame, his arms crossed over his chest. "I bet they have to put on more concerts when they release new dates, all because of the speculation on why they cancelled this time. They're trying to ramp up sales."

"Whatever," Lizzie said, waving him away. "I'm not surprised though. From what I heard, there's been trouble for a while."

"What sort of trouble?" Tess asked.

Lizzie shrugged and said, "It's all rumours of course, but their last album didn't sell as well as the first one."

"So?" Tess said.

"So, wouldn't you be unhappy if you were a popular band and you weren't selling your songs?"

"I guess so," Tess replied, though she really had no idea.

"You seem to know a lot about the band," Maddie said. She seemed to have gotten over her coughing fit.

"Lizzie's their number one fan," Will said.

"And the unofficial president of the unofficial fan club," Tess said.

Lizzie nodded and added, "I saw them on YouTube before they were famous."

"Really?" Maddie seemed a bit more interested now that she wasn't choking on tea.

"Yep. They only had a few hundred views on their videos when I first saw them, and then, out of nowhere, they just took off." Lizzie shot her hand in the air to emphasise the point.

"Wow, I never knew that," Maddie said.

"I'm not saying I deserve a cut of their profits or anything, but I can't help thinking that me sharing their videos and songs so much might have helped them get to where they are today."

Will laughed. "Did we tell you she's delusional?" He stepped over to the table, swiped the last piece of bacon from the tray and said, "I'd better get out there and start mowing before it gets too hot. I'll catch you all later."

Lizzie ignored him and continued. "I just think that bands need to reward their fans by, you know, not cancelling concerts out of the blue with no explanations."

"Maybe they just didn't want to play the music," Maddie said.

"Why?" Lizzie asked. "That's what people want to hear."

"But if they didn't sell their last album," Maddie said, shifting on her chair, "then maybe it was because people didn't like that music. And maybe the band didn't either."

Lizzie thought about that for a moment and said, "It shouldn't matter. Bands shouldn't annoy their fans like that."

"But shouldn't bands reward fans with great music? And if they don't think it's great music, why would they play it?"

"They shouldn't have recorded it in the first place and asked people to pay for it," Lizzie said simply.

"I guess so," Maddie replied.

"And don't you think it would be nice of them to actually reply to their fans on Twitter and Facebook or wherever once in a while instead of their agent or publicist or whoever does it?"

Maddie poked at the egg on her plate and there was an awkward silence, so Tess asked Lizzie, "Speaking of publicity, is your dad still going to put something in the paper for the festival?"

"I think so," Lizzie replied. She took a long drink of her orange juice. "I mean, he hasn't said anything, but he's done it every year. He's got some fancy photographer coming up to take some photos for the anniversary feature he's been talking about for months, so he's been a bit distracted."

"Can you ask him? We really need to do something special this year."

"I guess I could take some photos on my phone and see if he'll put them in with the article," Lizzie said. Tess didn't think Lizzie understood the gravity of the situation, but before she could explain any further, Gran bustled in and started clearing away the dishes.

"I want to get started on those cakes soon," she said, piling cups into plates and ferrying them into the kitchen. "Are you able to help today, Maddie?"

Maddie nodded. "I can help out for a few hours this morning, but I'm busy this afternoon."

Lizzie stood up and piled glasses and cutlery on a tray. "I have all day so I can help with whatever you need."

"You can help with the cupcakes," Tess said. She ferried the cereal boxes into the kitchen and offloaded them onto the bench. "We might get the afternoon off if we all get in and do them."

"Great," Lizzie said, taking the tray into the kitchen and stacking the glasses on the sink. "Can't wait."

As Tess filled up the sink and started washing the dishes, Gran began ferrying out the un-iced cupcakes. "I hope you've got your baking hat on Maddie," Tess heard her say. "We've got a lot more of these to do, and only a few days to do them."

Tess smiled. Even though she'd normally be the first to volunteer to be outside, she was looking forward to spending the morning with Maddie and Lizzie.

Eleven

AFTER A COUPLE OF hours of icing and packaging the baking, Maddie held up the limp piping bag in triumph and said, "Done." Tess looked up and laughed. Lizzie finished tying a ribbon around a clear cellophane bag that held four pieces of pink and white coconut ice and looked up.

"What's so funny?" Maddie asked.

"You've got icing everywhere," Tess said.

Maddie scrunched her nose and looked down at her hands, which were stained pink and blue. She looked back at Tess and smiled sheepishly. Tess threw her a hand towel and Maddie wiped her hands and face. "Gone?"

Tess nodded.

"Do we get to eat any of these as payment?" Maddie asked.

"Unfortunately, no. Gran makes us buy them on the weekend like everyone else," Tess replied.

"Really?"

"Afraid so," Lizzie confirmed.

"Well," Maddie said, tapping her chin with her finger. "Hypothetically, what would happen if one of the cupcakes just, you know, fell onto the floor?" She grinned mischievously, her hand poised above a newly-iced cupcake that sat perilously close to the edge of the table. Lizzie sucked in a breath.

"Well," said Tess. "You couldn't really sell it after that, could you? Hypothetically."

"Hypothetically," Maddie said and deftly flicked the cupcake off the table. Before Lizzie or Tess could jump up to retrieve it, Will appeared, seemingly from nowhere, scooped up the fallen cupcake, wiped off the top and shoved it into his mouth.

"Oops," he said, grinning.

Maddie laughed. "So not fair."

"You snooze, you lose," Will replied, licking the icing from his fingers. He peered into the kitchen and said, "Bloody hell. Is she feeding an army? It looks like Betty Crocker fired off a scattergun."

"You know what she's like with baking. Especially for the festival."

"What are you doing inside anyway?" Lizzie asked. "I thought you had a heap of stuff to do."

"Pop's let me go for today, but he's given me a list as long as both my arms to get to tomorrow."

"Are you sticking around for dinner?" Tess asked.

"Can't. Mum felt so bad about me missing out on the interview that she's making me a condolence dinner tonight."

"It's not like you missed out completely," Lizzie said.

"A condolence dinner?" Maddie asked.

"I missed out on a job interview," Will explained.

"Will's mum thinks food makes everything better," Tess said. "Kind of like Gran and baking."

"Oh," Maddie said.

"Yeah. She must feel really bad for me. She's making me Guinness Pie."

"Will's mum makes the best Guinness Pie in town," Tess said. "So good, that the Royal Hotel took it off the menu because Mrs Armstrong wouldn't give them her recipe, and people kept complaining that the pub's version wasn't as good as hers."

Maddie laughed.

"Do you think she'll make enough for leftovers?" Lizzie asked.

"Probably, but you could always just come for tea if you weren't doing anything."

Lizzie shrugged and said, "I guess so. Dad will be working on the paper and I think Mum's working a late shift tonight. I'll let you know."

"Cool," Will said. "I should get going. I've got some stuff to do for the band, but I'll be back in an hour or so." He swiped another cupcake off the table and walked away, winking at Maddie.

"I'll tell Gran on you," Tess teased.

Will called back, "I'm her favourite. She'll never believe you."

"He is Gran's favourite you know," Tess said to Maddie. "And he's not even really family."

"Who's my favourite?" Gran called from the kitchen.

"Will," Lizzie said.

Gran smiled. "He's a good boy, Will."

"Good Boy Will ate two of your cupcakes," Tess said.

"Oh, that doesn't matter. He's been working hard outside with Pop all morning."

"Does that mean we can have one?" Tess asked.

"Don't even think about it," Gran replied, swiping at Tess with a tea towel. She surveyed the table. "You girls have done a lot more than I thought you would. I'm impressed."

Maddie grinned. Even though it had been tough going, icing all those cupcakes, she'd had a good day. "I should get going," she said. "I have an appointment I need to get to, and I probably should have a shower and get changed."

"Thanks so much for helping," Gran said. "You're welcome for dinner tonight, if you're not busy."

"Thanks," Maddie said. "I'll check with Jo and let you know." She smiled as Tess helped her up and handed her the crutches.

"I'll walk you out," Tess said.

Maddie managed to hop her way down the three brick steps and turned to see Tess grinning at her. "I've had plenty of practice at the McGregor's," Maddie said.

Tess nodded and replied, "You looked a bit better than you did yesterday, trying to get down that one step at the bakery."

Maddie considered poking her tongue out, but she thought Tess might think it childish if she did it twice in two days. So she just wiggled her head and said, "Ha ha."

"I'll see you later?" Tess asked.

"I hope so," Maddie replied. She knew that coming to Tess's for dinner later would hinge on how her phone call went this afternoon so she didn't want to make any promises.

Twelve

AFTER MAKING A START on the Cow Pat Bingo field, Tess and Lizzie decided it was far too hot to be working outside. Gran and Pop had gone into town to take the cupcakes to the bakery to store until the weekend, and Will had just arrived back after spending some time with his band.

They'd all just moved down a few metres on the front veranda chasing the shade, and Tess lay back on the banana lounge listening to Lizzie and Will discussing the cancelled concerts again.

"Listen to this," Lizzie said, reading out yet another update. "Someone who says they're close to the band says that Indiana Rose has definitely gone to rehab."

"And they know this how?" Will asked. He was bent over the screen on his tablet sorting out his band's playlist for the weekend.

"He's been around for ages, like me. He always seems to know what's going on."

"Sounds like a snitch," Will said. "Or an idiot who wants everyone to think he knows the band."

"Doesn't matter," Lizzie replied. "At least someone seems to be telling us all what's going on."

"What does it matter?" Will asked. "The concerts were cancelled. Why do you need to know why?"

"Enquiring minds want to know, and I need to have something to write on my blog next week."

Though Lizzie wanted to be a proper journalist, she spent a lot of time maintaining her fan blog for the band. It was mainly just gossip and a place for her to chat to other fans, but she took it very seriously.

"Speaking of gossip," Will said. "I overheard Pop tell Gran that the council wasn't going to stump up any money this year. What's that about?"

"Who knows?" Tess said. "But it's got Pop worried. He says they've had stallholders pull out too, so it's not looking good. He even said we might not have a festival next year."

"Really?" Lizzie looked up from her phone.

Tess nodded forlornly. "Not much we can do he reckons."

"I don't know," Will said. "I reckon there's plenty we can do."

"Like what?" Tess asked.

"You know what," Will said.

Tess shook her head. "Pop won't go for it, Will. He won't let us get more bands than we have—"

"Which is how many exactly?" Lizzie asked.

Tess sat up. "Look, we just need to get through this year, and then we'll have a whole year to come up with something better."

"We have come up with something better," Will said. "We could talk to Pop—"

"No," Tess said, sliding her feet off the chair and onto the floor. "I told you, Pop said no, and when he makes up his mind, there's no changing it."

"I just don't get it," Will said. "Don't you want to save the festival?"

"Of course I do," Tess said. "But it's way too late now to be making changes. It's only a couple of days away."

Will picked at the cover on his tablet. Lizzie, obviously sensing the tension, said, "I can see if Dad can do a bit more of a feature in the paper on Friday."

"Would you?" Tess asked.

"Sure. Why not?" Lizzie said. "A bit of extra publicity might make more people come on the weekend."

"Power of the press, hey?" Will said.

"Yep," Lizzie said. "And that's exactly my point about the band. They could've done a press conference, or released a statement or—"

"God, Lizzie, you can turn anything back on to talking about Three's Company," Will said, throwing himself melodramatically back into his beanbag.

Lizzie went quiet as she scrolled through her phone. She'd do that for ages, just trolling for bits of information on the band.

Tess let her mind wander and wondered what Maddie was doing. Maddie had messaged earlier to let Tess know that she had another appointment in the morning but didn't say whether she'd be able to come to dinner or not.

As if he'd read Tess's mind, Will asked, "What's Maddie up to this afternoon?"

"Not sure," Tess said. "She had an appointment but I'm not sure what else."

Lizzie said, "We should see what she's up to this afternoon. See if she wants to come over."

"And do what? We're not exactly doing anything exciting," Tess said.

"We could watch a movie," Lizzie suggested.

"We just spent all morning inside," Tess replied.

"We could go swimming up at the dam," Will said. He gave Tess a little smile.

Tess smiled back and said, "That's a great idea."

Will stood up and stretched. "Text Maddie and see if she wants to come. She can show Lizzie how she won judge's choice last night."

Tess laughed and said, "She won't be sneaking that past me again." She took out her phone and sent Maddie a text. While she waited for

Maddie's reply, Lizzie said, "You know, Maddie kind of reminds me of someone, but I can't quite put my finger on it."

"She kind of looks like that actress," Will said. "What's her name? From Mercury Point."

"Tiffany McDonald?" Tess guessed. Tiffany would be the only one Will was referring to since she was another of his unattainable crushes. Come to think of it, Maddie did look a little like Tiffany. Though Tiffany had longer hair, and it was darker with a thick red streak through her fringe.

"That's her," Will confirmed.

"Maybe," Lizzie said, "but I don't think that's it."

Tess's phone buzzed. Maddie replied Will ask Jo Give me 10.

"What did she say?" Will asked.

"She has to ask Jo," Tess said. She stood up and wandered over to the edge of the veranda and leaned on the railing.

"I'll go get us some towels," Lizzie said and headed inside.

Thirteen

THE FACT THAT THE phone was Jo's was the only thing that had saved it from being smashed to pieces. Maddie had decided, obviously against her better judgement, to call her father just to let him know she was fine and Jo had agreed to let her use her phone because Maddie was paranoid her father could trace her own. She hadn't been talking with him for more than ten minutes and it had turned into another raging argument about her future. More than ever she felt like her life wasn't her own anymore, and that her opinions and choices didn't matter.

Jo had let her rant and rave without interruption, and when Maddie had finally calmed down, Jo had suggested they go into town to get out of the house. Maddie had refused, but Jo had gone in any way to get some groceries, leaving Maddie to quietly fume on her own. What was it with her father and wanting to be so controlling? He never used to be like that. Did he? Her mother maybe, but not her dad. He'd been on her side when she was little but then everything changed when they had more money than they knew what to do with. It was great at first. She had a wardrobe other girls her age would kill for and a house straight out of a magazine. It hadn't taken long for her parents to become a lot more restrictive about everything from what she wore to what she ate. It seemed like every time she turned around, her choices were totally ignored in favour of what her parents wanted.

Despite Maddie's initial reservations, Jo bringing her to Chesterfield for a break had ended up being one of her best ideas. Being away from her family and away from the pressures of her life had given her some perspective. She still had no idea what to do about her life though, and she didn't know how much longer she'd be allowed to stay away before the rumours really kicked into overdrive.

She walked to the top of the stairs on the front veranda of the farmhouse and leaned her head against a post. She was looking out across the cane field, wondering what she was going to do about her life now that she realised how far she'd fallen when she got a text message. It was Tess.

Going swimming at the dam. Want to come?

Maddie looked up toward the farmhouse. Sure enough, though she couldn't see clearly, she could just make out a couple of people on the veranda. She wasn't sure Jo would let her out of the house given her latest outburst, but it wouldn't hurt to ask. She replied to Tess, telling her to give her ten minutes to ask Jo.

Then she sent her another text.

Is that you on the veranda?

Yes. How do you know?

Can see you.

The person on the veranda, who Maddie now knew was Tess, waved. Maddie waved back.

I can see you too What are you up to?

Maddie considered her answer. Considering my future.

That's a bit deep. Tess replied.

Maddie laughed in spite of herself. You haven't thought about your future?

Nope. What's to think about? Finish school, go to uni, get a job Simple.

Maddie looked up. Tess had moved down to the closest corner, and Maddie could see it was definitely Tess now.

Maddie text back My life's not so simple.

You're on holiday. How complicated can it be?

Maddie shook her head. She wished she could explain her situation to Tess but she didn't know how to. Let's just say I have lots to think about.

Want to talk about it?

Maddie sighed. She wasn't sure what else there was to say, but maybe talking to someone who didn't know about her situation could give her some perspective. She text back Yeah maybe I'm not sure.

K Here if you need.

Maddie looked over at the farmhouse. She imagined Tess standing there, her blond hair tied back, loose strands falling across her face like they had that morning when she'd been concentrating so intently on icing the cupcakes. Not that she'd been watching Tess too closely. She wondered if Tess knew she stuck her tongue out the side of her mouth when she concentrated. Maddie smiled at the memory and text back Thanks.

How's your graze?

Scab off. Skin is very pink.

That's good. How about your ankle?

Bruising looks worse than it is. Starting to go yellow.

It'll be gone in a day or two.

The bruise or my ankle?

Haha, I meant the bruise.

Maddie smiled. Dr let me get rid of my extra legs :)

But four legs suit you :-p

Oh so funny. Glad to have my own two back.

Heading off now. Last chance. A swim might clear your head. Can come get you if your ankle is still sore :)

Maddie smiled. She could certainly do with the distraction but she had no idea when Jo would be back. She could just call Jo she supposed, but then that would give her a chance to say no. Instead, she replied to Tess's text with I'll see you in 5. And then she sent Jo a text that said Gone swimming with Tess. Might stay for dinner.

Tess decided to take Maddie up to the dam on Chitty, the old VW Beetle that'd had all the panelling taken off. It used to be the farm vehicle of choice, but it didn't get used much any more thanks to getting harder and harder to start. Thankfully though, it didn't embarrass Tess today by deciding to be stubborn and they made it to the dam just in time to see Will launching himself off the rope swing and into the water near the treehouse.

"You didn't tell me you had a treehouse," Maddie said as she pulled herself out of the seat.

"Pretty cool, huh?" Tess said.

"Very," Maddie said. Tess helped her limp over to the old pontoon that was tied to the bank of the dam and lowered her down onto a towel. She doubled back to retrieve the Esky and put it down on the bank beside the pontoon.

Lizzie was sitting cross-legged on a towel, her phone in her hand. Tess shook her head. "Can you put that down for one minute?"

"I'm just welcoming the new followers," Lizzie said. "The post only went live this morning and already it's been retweeted over a hundred times."

"Can we expect to have you in the real world any time soon?" Tess asked.

"Just give me one minute," Lizzie said, her thumbs working furiously over her screen.

Will swam closer and splashed at Lizzie, who pulled her phone away and scowled at him. "You break it, you buy me a new one."

"If you don't put it away, I'll drag you into the dam," Will said.

Lizzie narrowed her eyes but put her phone into her bag. "There. Satisfied?"

"Very," Will said. "Now are you girls coming swimming or not?"

Tess looked at Maddie and said, "Do you want to go in?"

"In a minute," Maddie said. "I'll just watch you guys for a bit."

"Suit yourself," Tess said. She pulled off her t-shirt, dropped it beside Maddie, and then walked up the bank and over to the tree where the rope swing hung. She took hold of the rope and pulled it to her. "See how far you can get?" she called to Will.

"Okay. But don't be a sook when I beat your ass again," Will replied.

Tess laughed and launched herself off the bank. She waited until she was at the top of the swing and let go. She flailed in the air, just for effect, and splashed into the brown dam water. When she surfaced, she shook her head and wiped her face. Will was already climbing back up the bank, so Tess swam across to give him some room.

He took hold of the rope, pulled it back as far as it would let him, and took a running jump off the bank. He let go and splashed down beside Tess. When he surfaced he looked at Tess and seeing he hadn't beaten her said, "Best of three?"

"You're on," Tess said.

Maddie watched as Will and Tess tried to best each other off the rope swing. She didn't really want to go swimming in the dam. She had a thing about swimming in water where she couldn't see the bottom and hoped Tess wouldn't push her to get in.

"Bloody show-offs," Lizzie said. She stood up, pulled off her shorts, and dropped them onto her towel. "Are you coming in?"

Maddie shook her head. "Nah. I'll just watch."

"Time to show those two how it's done," Lizzie said. She walked over to the rope swing and called, "Amateurs." She took hold of the rope and pulled it back. As she ran towards the edge of the bank, her foot slipped in the grass and she careened off the edge. Instead of swinging out into the dam like Will and Tess had, Lizzie screamed as she skidded across the top of the water before she finally let go of the rope. She surfaced, coughing and spluttering and Maddie couldn't help but laugh.

"I meant that," Lizzie said, as she swam over to Will and Tess.

Maddie watched as the three of them splashed around and dunked each other and thought about Freya and Andy. They were the only friends she had at that moment who knew the real Maddie. Though she could picture Andy jumping off a rope swing into muddy brown water, there was no way Freya would even put a toe in a dam. Despite everything that had happened over the last few months, the two constants in Maddie's life had been Freya and Andy. And Jo, if she was honest, but Jo was a different story altogether. Though she was glad she'd decided to take a break from her hectic life, she decided that calling Freya and talking to her about some of the things that had been running through her head would help her decide what to do next. She needed to talk to her about where they were headed and whether they were all still even on the same page.

Tess swam over and rested her arms on the pontoon. "Sure you don't want to come in?"

"I'm quite happy watching you guys show off," Maddie said, nodding over to where Will and Lizzie were trying to dunk each other.

"It's not often we have someone to show off to," Tess said.

Maddie found herself blushing. She looked down at the towel she was sitting on and smiled.

"Hey," Tess said. "You want to see the treehouse? It's probably cooler in there."

Maddie looked up. "I'd love to."

"Great," Tess said. She pulled herself up onto the pontoon, and Maddie bit her lip as she watched the water drip down Tess's legs. Tess wrapped a towel around her waist and held out her hand. She lifted Maddie to her feet and Maddie didn't mind a bit that Tess holding her so close to help her over to the treehouse made her clothes wet.

Fourteen

"WOW," MADDIE SAID AS she ducked through the doorway. "This is really cool. I always wanted a treehouse."

"Sorry about the dust," Tess said. "We haven't been up here since September so we haven't cleaned it up in a while."

"Do you come up here a lot?" Maddie asked, limping over to the open window on the far side. She leaned out and waved to Will and Lizzie who were laying on the pontoon drying out.

"Not as much as when we were kids. We used to come up here with chips and soft drinks and play cards. Sometimes we'd bring up sleeping bags and stay overnight. We haven't done that in ages though."

"It's a great view," Maddie said, leaning further out of the window.

"Check this out," Tess said. She pushed open the skylight she'd installed with Will a few years ago and propped it up with a piece of wood.

"Can you see the stars through that?" Maddie asked, standing underneath it and looking up.

"You can when it gets dark," Tess said.

Maddie sneezed and shook her head. "Something dropped on me." She went to wipe it away but Tess realised what it was a second before Maddie smeared black across her face.

Tess grabbed Maddie's hand and said, "Wait." She licked a finger on her other hand and pressed it lightly onto the black piece of cane trash that had landed on Maddie's cheek just below her eye. Tess managed to take it off without it crumbling and showed Maddie under the light. "See? It's a piece of cane trash. Black snow."

"Black snow," Maddie repeated, peering at it.

"Yeah, from cane fires. It was probably caught up in the skylight."

Maddie looked up from the cane trash on Tess's finger and into Tess's eyes and her breath caught in her throat. Tess blinked and wiped her hand off on her shorts and turned away. "Do you want a drink?" she asked. "We brought some up in the Esky."

"Sure," Maddie said.

"I'll be right back," Tess said and disappeared through the doorway.

Maddie looked around at the weathered wood and old crates and cushions scattered around. Her mother would never let her have anything like this when she was a kid. Her father definitely wouldn't have been able to make her one. If she'd insisted on having a treehouse, they would have ordered it from a catalogue, or in more recent years, had it built specially. It certainly would not have been built out of old bits of wood and doors, like this one was. The fact that the corners weren't square, and the roof leaked little shafts of light made Maddie feel at ease.

When Tess came back, she was holding two cups and had a plastic container tucked under her arm. She handed a cup to Maddie and said, "I hope you like ginger beer. Pop makes it himself."

Maddie took a cup and said, "Thanks." She took a sip and smiled. Tess sat down on one of the crates and pulled one out for Maddie. Maddie sat down and Tess watched as she looked around at the treehouse. It wasn't much and she really hoped Maddie would look past the recycled windows and wood.

"You're so lucky growing up in a place like this," Maddie said.

"In a treehouse?"

Maddie laughed. "No. In Chesterfield. It's so... quiet."

Outside, Will whooped and there was a splash and then a squeal from Lizzie. Maddie and Tess both laughed.

"Not too quiet," Tess said, shifting her weight so she could curl her foot up underneath her.

"There's nothing wrong with quiet. My life is so busy. So... noisy."

"Is that what you've been thinking about?"

"What do you mean?"

"The texts from earlier. Thinking about your life."

"I guess," Maddie said. "Do you ever wonder where you're heading?"

Tess shrugged. "Not a lot. I knew from when I was little that I'd have to leave Chesterfield to go to uni if I didn't want to end up working behind a counter at the bakery for the rest of my life."

Maddie sighed. "I'd give anything to be so sure of where I'm heading. Maybe I should have grown up in a small town."

"It's not that great," Tess said.

"From where I'm sitting, it's a lot better than where I've grown up."

"It's okay for a while," Tess said. "When you're a kid growing up, there's heaps to do. Now? The cinema closed a few months ago and apart from some workshops the council puts on in school holidays, there's really not much else to do outside of school."

"Which is why you like the festival so much?"

Tess nodded. "I love coming out here to help Pop and Gran set up and get the place ready. It's my happy place."

Maddie laughed into her cup.

"What? Too cheesy?"

"No," Maddie said, shaking her head. "Everyone has to have their happy place."

"Where's yours?" Tess asked.

Maddie turned away and looked out the window. She sighed and said, "You know, I'm not really sure anymore."

Tess thought back to their text conversation from earlier. She wondered what could be weighing so heavily on Maddie's mind that she couldn't talk about it. "I'm happy to share my happy place," Tess said.

When Maddie turned back, she was smiling. "I'd like that." She sipped her drink and said, "You know, I asked a lady at a cafe when I was in town about the festival."

"Oh?"

"Yeah. She kinda said it wasn't worth going to."

"Oh."

"Sorry."

Tess shrugged. "Don't be."

"What's the deal with that?"

"The locals? It's been the same every year I guess. Same rides, same stalls, same Cow Pat Bingo."

"I can't wait to see how Cow Pat Bingo works," Maddie said.

"There's nothing to it," Tess replied. "You just pick a number, pay whatever ransom Lonny is asking for and wait to see if Bessie poos on it."

Maddie laughed.

"What number would you pick?" Tess asked. "Between one and a hundred."

"My favourite number is seven," Maddie said.

"Not a bad number. Seven figures highly in Bessie's pooing patterns."

"Really?"

"Yeah. Except she prefers numbers like twenty-seven or fifty-seven." Tess sipped her drink.

"I'll have to think about it and get back to you on Saturday." Maddie chewed on the side of her cup and said, "What about bands? Didn't you say you had bands that played at the festival?"

Tess snorted. "Yeah. Well. Will's band is headlining this year because they're the best we have."

"What are they called?"

"The Trojan Kings."

"Cool name," Maddie said.

"Dexter, their drummer, came up with it. He saw the name on a condom packet."

Maddie tossed her head back and laughed. It was loud and spontaneous and hearing it made Tess smile. "I've heard some funny stories about band names but that one's pretty good," Maddie said.

"Will didn't like it to start off with but it just seemed to stick."

"What type of music do they play?" Maddie asked.

"Rock and a bit of metal," Tess said. "Covers mostly. They tried playing some of their own stuff last year, but it didn't go down so well."

"Tough crowd."

"Yeah."

"So no big-name acts this year?"

"We haven't got the money to pay the bigger bands from the city to come up. We used to, but not anymore."

"Pity," Maddie said. "Small music festivals are the best to go to."

"Do you like music festivals?"

"I love them," Maddie said. She missed being able to go to them whenever she wanted to. "There tends to be a lot where I'm from."

"And where's that?"

"Sydney mainly."

"Mainly? How can you be mainly from Sydney?"

Maddie sighed. "I travel around a lot."

"Your parents move for work?"

Maddie looked across to the window again and Tess wondered if she'd touched a nerve. "Sort of," Maddie said finally, after a long silence.

Tess felt like Maddie wasn't telling her everything, but she didn't want to push her. She was curious about Maddie and her life and where she'd come from and why she was in Chesterfield, but maybe Maddie would tell her when she was ready.

"I bet that sucks," Tess said. "Moving around a lot."

Maddie smiled and said, "Yeah. It does."

Tess got the feeling that she should change the subject, so she said, "I have a surprise for you. Do you want to see it?"

Maddie's eyes lit up and she said excitedly, "Of course!"

Tess handed Maddie the container she'd brought in when she'd gotten the drinks. Maddie took it and peeked under the lid. She took in a sharp breath and said, "You stole a cupcake."

"I wouldn't have done it for anyone else."

Maddie took the lid from the container and lifted the cupcake out like it was something precious. "Only one though?"

"You have no idea how hard it was to just get that one," Tess said.

"We can share it if you like," Maddie said. She gently pulled the paper wrapper from the side of the cake.

"You have it," Tess said. "I got it for you."

Maddie took a bite and giggled when cake crumbs dropped onto her lap. "I've been waiting to eat one of these all day," she said. "It was so worth the wait."

"I'm glad you like it."

Maddie waggled the uneaten half in front of Tess and said, "Last chance."

Tess shook her head. "It's all yours."

Maddie grinned as she devoured the rest of the cupcake and then licked the icing and crumbs from her fingers. "That was so good," she said, leaning back against the tree house wall with a contented sigh.

The sun had started to go down, throwing orange light in through the window. From where Tess was sitting, it looked like Maddie had the slightest hint of a halo on the top of her head. Maddie turned and looked back at Tess. When she saw Tess looking at her, she smiled back. It made Tess's heart leap. She swallowed hard and they sat there for what felt like ages. Then something flickered over Maddie's face and she sat up. She looked down and played with the cuff of her shorts. When she looked up, it seemed like she was about to say something, but whatever it was, she was interrupted by Will thudding up the treehouse ladder. "Fire," he said, breathing hard.

"What?"

"There's a fire near the house. We have to go." He disappeared back outside.

Tess leaped up and when she reached the door she looked toward the farmhouse. In the distance, black smoke was curling up into the sky on the southern side of the house. "Oh no," Tess said.

"What's wrong?" Maddie asked, peering over Tess's shoulder.

"That looks like the festival block." Tess turned and climbed down the ladder. She helped Maddie down and they raced over to Chitty.

Will and Lizzie were waiting on one of the farm bikes. "We'll meet you there," Will called over the roar of the engine and he took off up the track, red dust billowing out behind him.

Maddie climbed into the passenger seat beside Tess, who turned the engine over. Chitty spluttered to life and Tess tore up the track after Will.

Fifteen

BY THE TIME THEY'd made it back to the house, the cane field that had been saved for the festival was well alight. There were people everywhere trying to get it under control and when Tess went to see if she could help, Will stopped her. "It's gone, Tess."

Tess knew he was right. She slumped against him for a moment and then together, they trudged up the stairs to stand on the veranda next to Gran, Maddie, and Lizzie. Tess watched in horror as the fire roared through the cane and over the noise, she heard Pop yell, "Let it go. It's gone." Gran sighed and turned and walked inside.

"That was pretty spectacular," Maddie said.

"Yeah," was all Tess could manage to say in reply.

"That's what was supposed to happen on the weekend?" Maddie asked.

"Yep," Tess said. She wasn't sure what they'd do now. With no big-name bands and hardly any stallholders, the cane fire was the last big thing they had to draw in crowds to the festival.

Maddie curled her fingers into Tess's and squeezed. "I'm so sorry, Tess."

"I'm going to see if Gran needs a hand inside," Lizzie said.

"I'll go and see if Pop needs anything," Will said. He gave Tess's shoulder a squeeze as he walked past and headed downstairs. Tess watched him as he climbed over the fence and walked over to where Pop and a few of the other locals had gathered in a group. She tried desperately not to cry.

Maddie leaned into Tess's shoulder and they watched as Pop, Will and the others mopped up and put out the small grass fires around the block. One by one, they walked up the driveway and onto the veranda, kicked off their blackened boots, and went inside.

Pop and Will were the last ones to come up. Pop, exhausted and his face covered in black soot, patted Tess on the arm and said, "Come inside and get something to eat."

"In a minute," Tess said.

Pop gave her a tired smile and said, "Don't be too long."

"I won't."

Pop trudged inside after Will. Normally, the conversation from inside after a fire was loud and raucous. Normally, it was exhilarating and exciting, but not this time. This time, it was quiet.

"We should get inside," Maddie said.

"You don't have to stay," Tess said. "We'll all just be down in the dumps anyway."

"That's okay," Maddie said. Her phone rang and when she pulled it out of her pocket, she said to Tess, "It's Jo." Tess nodded. "Hi Jo," Maddie said. "I'm at Tess's, why?" She sighed. "No, I'm fine. It was the cane near the house... Well, what time will you be home?" She pulled a face at Tess, and Tess smiled. Maddie sighed and rolled her eyes. "Fine. I'm staying with Tess for a bit and then I'll be home... I'll get something to eat here so don't worry about me... Okay. Sure... Yes. Okay, okay, I won't be late. Bye." She hung up and said to Tess, "She heard about the fire in town. Does news always travel that fast around here?"

Tess nodded and said, "Yep. You have no idea." She took Maddie's hand and led her inside.

Though Gran had piled the dining table high with food, not much of it was getting eaten. Even Pete's nephew didn't seem to be hungry. Tess wasn't hungry either, but she nibbled on a ham sandwich because there wasn't anything else she felt she could do. Finally, Lonny broke the silence. "Looks like it started down the bottom corner," he said.

Pop grunted in reply.

"Any idea what started it?" Will asked. He poured himself a glass of water and had a long drink.

"Doesn't matter," Pop said. He bit into a sandwich and brushed the crumbs from his chin.

"Why not?" Tess asked.

"Because the festival's not going ahead," Pop said quietly.

"What? No!" Tess dropped the remains of her sandwich on her plate.

"Tess," Gran warned, but Tess wasn't listening.

"Just because the block's gone doesn't mean we have to cancel the festival."

"It's not just the block," Pop said. "There's no money to pay for it."

"But the council—"

Pete scoffed. "Bloody council don't want to know about it." He dipped his biscuit into his tea and bit off the end.

Tess was confused. She knew the council wasn't going to give them as much as last year, but they were at least going to give them something. Weren't they?

"The council are giving us some money, aren't they?" Tess asked.

"There is no money," Pop fumed. "There's no money from the council, and we haven't got any spare. So that's it. The festival's done."

Tess pushed herself away from the table so hard that her chair fell over backwards and clattered to the floor. "That's crap," she said. "You can't just cancel it. What about all the people who are coming?"

Pop's face reddened. "There are no people," he said. "We've got no stalls and now we've got no reason for people to come." He stood up, placed both his hands on the table, looked down at the floor, and took a deep breath. "The festival's cancelled, and that's that." Before Tess could protest any more, Pop left the dining room and went out to the laundry. She wanted to race after him and plead with him to reconsider, but when she heard the back door slam, she knew it would be useless. He was doing what he always did when he needed to calm down which was to go and tinker in the old shed, and if she tried to change his mind while he was still angry, she'd only make things worse.

Gran stood up and said, "Thanks everyone for helping out tonight at short notice. Maddie, you should probably get home. You too," she said to Will and Lizzie.

"Come on," Lizzie said, taking Tess's arm. "Walk us out."

Tess let Lizzie lead her back out to the front veranda with Will and Maddie trailing behind.

"I can't believe it's over, just like that," Tess said. She leaned on the veranda railing and covered her face with her hands.

"I'm sure Pop's just angry," Will said, giving Tess a rub on her shoulder. "Let him cool off a bit and we'll see what he says tomorrow."

Tess wasn't so sure, but Will was right about one thing. It was useless trying to talk to Pop now when he was upset and being totally unreasonable. Lizzie wrapped Tess in a hug and said, "We'll catch up tomorrow."

Tess nodded.

"I should probably get home too," Maddie said. "Do you want to walk me back?"

"Yeah," Tess said. They waved to Lizzie and Will as they left in Will's ute and watched as the taillights disappeared around the corner. Maddie took Tess's hand and said, "Come on. Some fresh air will do you good."

The fact that Maddie held Tess's hand on the walk to the McGregor house dulled some of the pain Tess felt over the cane fire. They stopped at the bottom of the steps and Maddie turned to face Tess. She glanced at the ground and when she looked back up, her face was half in shadow. Tess thought she looked like a photo taken in soft focus.

"I don't think I've ever been on such an eventful date," Maddie said quietly.

"I didn't realise it was a date," Tess said.

Maddie looked down at the ground. "Well, you know what I mean."

Tess didn't know what Maddie meant, but she didn't question it.

"I'm sorry about the festival," Maddie said. She took Tess's hand and held it, rubbing her thumb over the back of Tess's hand, sending shivers up Tess's arm.

Tess blew out a breath and said, "Yeah. I'm not sure what we're going to do now."

"Well, I know it's probably not much of a consolation, but if Pop does cancel the festival, maybe we could do something. Just you and me."

"I'd like that," Tess said. She wiped her hand across her face and said, "I'm sorry you had to hear all of that stuff back at the house."

"What stuff?" Maddie asked.

"Me and Pop arguing."

Maddie squeezed Tess's hand and said, "The festival obviously means a lot to you both."

"Yeah," Tess said. She looked down at the ground, unsure what else there was to say.

Before either of them could say any more, the downstairs light flicked on.

"Jo," Maddie sighed.

"I should go," Tess said.

"And I should go before Jo comes down, guns blazing."

"Would she do that?" Tess asked, glancing nervously up at the doorway.

Maddie laughed and leaned in and kissed Tess on the cheek. Tess desperately resisted the urge to reach up and touch the spot where Maddie's lips had touched her skin. "At least I got to eat that cupcake," Maddie whispered into Tess's ear as she pulled away. Her breath on Tess's cheek gave her goosebumps. Maddie squeezed Tess's hand and said, "I'll see you tomorrow."

Tess waited until Maddie had walked up the stairs. When she reached the top she turned and waved. Tess waved back and walked back to the farm, feeling better than she should about the way the day had ended up.

Sixteen

MADDIE WAS UP EARLIER than usual the next morning after tossing and turning the night before. She went out and stood on the front veranda to look out on the cane field that had burned last night. Yesterday, when she and Jo had been out there after Maddie's argument with her father, the cane field was thick and green and swished in the breeze. Today, it looked like a blackened wasteland.

This morning Maddie had watched as Tess trudged down the steps of the veranda, walked over to the cane field, and sat down on the grass. She leaned against the corner fence post, picking at the ground. Maddie was wondering whether she should go and talk to her when Jo came out and handed her a cup of tea. She stood beside Maddie and sipped on her coffee.

"Pretty devastating," Jo said.

"Yeah."

"Any idea what happened?"

Maddie shrugged. "I didn't stay around long enough to find out." Maddie cupped her hands around her teacup and watched as Tess threw something into the cane.

"You should go and talk to her," Jo said.

"I don't know what to say," Maddie replied. What did you say to someone whose festival just got ruined last night?

"Just go and see how she is," Jo said.

"She probably doesn't want to talk to anyone," Maddie said, sipping on her tea. "She was pretty upset last night. Besides, what can I do? I can't bring the cane back."

"She might feel better having slept on it last night," Jo said. "Anyway, sometimes just knowing you have someone to make sure you're okay is enough."

Maddie knew Jo was right. She handed Jo her teacup and said, "I'll be back soon."

"Don't forget you've got that Skype call in an hour," Jo said as she opened the screen door. "And we should probably get there a bit early. I'm not sure what the internet's like out here."

Maddie nodded and headed down the stairs.

Tess shielded her eyes when she looked up and was pleased to see it was Maddie. "Hey," she said.

"Hey," Maddie said and sat down on the grass beside Tess. "How are you doing?"

Tess shrugged. "Okay."

"Any idea what happened?"

Tess shook her head. "Lonny reckons it was Barry Montgomery or someone else from the council."

"Really? They'd sabotage you like that?"

"I don't know," Tess said. She threw a rock into the cane. "It doesn't matter now though, does it?"

"Pop wouldn't really cancel the festival would he?"

Tess sniffed. "I don't know. I haven't spoken to Pop today. He was gone super early this morning and Gran's not sure when he'll be back."

Maddie placed her hand on Tess's. "I'm sorry, Tess. We'll work something out."

Tess sighed. "That's what everyone keeps saying, but no-one seems to know what 'something' actually is."

Maddie didn't respond and Tess realised that she probably didn't need to speak the way she had. She turned her hand over and intertwined her fingers with Maddie's.

Maddie squeezed back. "You know what? We should do something today."

"Like what?"

Maddie shrugged. "I'm sure we could come up with something."

"In case you hadn't noticed," Tess said, "this is Chesterfield. There's nothing to do in Chesterfield."

"Well," Maddie said. "We could just meet in town and see if we can find something to keep us busy."

"I don't know," Tess said, prodding at the ground with her free hand. "I don't really feel like doing anything at the moment." She tossed another rock into the blackened cane. She knew that Maddie was trying to lighten the mood and get her mind off of last night's fire, but the fire and the festival were all Tess could think about.

"What else have you got planned for today?" Maddie asked. "Apart from moping around about the fire?"

Tess pulled a face and replied, "Nothing. We were meant to start setting stuff up today, but Gran said to hold off."

"I have an appointment this morning and nothing on this afternoon. What about we meet for lunch?"

Tess thought about it for a second and though she wanted to have lunch with Maddie and spend more time with her, she didn't want to miss talking to Pop when she finally had the chance. She said, "Thanks for the offer, but I'd just be a wet blanket."

"Are you sure?" Maddie said.

"Yeah," Tess said. "Sorry."

Maddie checked her watch. "I have to get going. I'll call by later if that's okay and we can just hang out." She let go of Tess's hand and stood up.

Tess stood up too and shoved her hands into her pockets. "I guess."

Maddie smiled and said, "I'll see you later."

"Okay," Tess said. She leaned on the fence post, watching Maddie walk back to the McGregor's. When Maddie reached the bottom of the steps she turned and waved. Tess waved back and, taking one last look at the blackened stalks of cane, she went back inside to have breakfast.

Seventeen

MADDIE SAT AT THE conference table, the laptop in front of her, waiting for the Skype call to come through. She'd run into Will and Lizzie in town that morning and between them, they'd all decided Tess needed to get out of the house. All three of them had tried and failed multiple times to get Tess to answer her phone, and it was Will who'd come up with the idea of staging an intervention and taking Tess up to the treehouse to force her to have some fun. Though Maddie wasn't entirely sure whether it would work or not she was up for the challenge. When Lizzie said she had to work on the paper with her dad and Will suddenly remembered he had band practice, Maddie wasn't so sure she could pull it off herself.

"Tess likes you," Will had said when Maddie questioned whether Tess would even come if it was just the two of them. Hearing the words that confirmed what Maddie thought she was feeling from Tess had given her butterflies. Will had also offered to go up to the treehouse to help Maddie clean it up a bit since it was still full of dust. She'd have sworn Will was trying to set her and Tess up on a date, but since she didn't know Will all that well, she'd give him the benefit of the doubt. Besides, asking Tess on a date was what Maddie had tried to do this morning. What would it matter if it was a setup?

The laptop screen lit up as the call came through and when Maddie answered it, Freya appeared trying to wrestle her wild curls into a scarf.

"Hey stranger," Freya said.

"Hey. How's things?" Maddie asked.

"Good," Freya said. She peered closer at the screen. "Have you changed your hair?"

"What do you think?" Maddie turned her head left and then right so Freya could see it properly.

Freya whistled. "It's different," she said.

"You don't like it?"

"I didn't say that," Freya said. "I'm just so used to seeing it longer and blonder, that's all."

"I just, you know, wanted a change."

"Some change," Freya said. "How do you feel about it?"

Maddie shrugged. "I like it. I haven't had short hair since I was little. It's freeing being able to get up in the morning and just put a hat on."

"Ha! I wish I knew what that was like," Freya said shaking her head and loosening some of the curls that had so far managed to stay put in the scarf.

Maddie laughed and said, "Have you seen Andy?"

Freya threw her head back and laughed. "Are you kidding? All I've had from Andy have been a couple of pictures of girls at the beach and a text that said 'surf's gnarly'."

Maddie laughed. "Yeah. He sent the same ones to me. I'm glad he's having some fun."

"I think we all needed to let off some steam after the last few months," Freya said. "Speaking of, have you spoken to your dad?"

"No," Maddie lied. "Have you?"

Freya made a face. "Yeah. He's gone back to Sydney. He's not happy with Andy and me. He thinks we know where you are but won't tell him."

"Sorry," Maddie said. "Has he said anything?"

"About what?"

"About why I left."

Freya shrugged. "He's trying to put out spot fires. You know what he's like. All business."

"Yeah," Maddie said. "That's why I left."

"As long as he's dealing with business, he's leaving us alone," Freya said.

"Yeah," Maddie agreed absently. "So you're okay? With everything that happened?"

Freya shrugged. "I have to be. You weren't happy, man, and blind Freddy could've seen it. I'm surprised you took so long to crack."

Maddie laughed. Typical, easy-going Freya. "As long as you're not mad."

"Why would I be mad?"

"I walked out on you guys," Maddie said.

Freya shrugged. "None of us were happy, and you were the only one with the balls to say something."

"Yeah but I might've stuffed everything up," Maddie replied. The last thing she'd wanted when she'd left was to leave Freya and Andy in the lurch.

"Nah. It's all good. Everyone needs a break at some point. We'll be fine. Don't worry about it."

Maddie wasn't so sure and she wished she could share Freya's optimism.

"Hey, check this out," Freya said, leaning away from the screen. When she popped her head back up, she produced a square piece of wool with a hole in the middle and knitting needles sticking out of the sides.

"What is that?" Maddie asked.

"It's a scarf," Freya said. "Part of one at least. Can't you tell?"

Maddie squinted at the screen and said, "You missed a bit."

Freya stuck a finger through the hole and said, "I'm still getting the hang of it."

"I didn't know you knitted," Maddie said.

"I do now."

"Why?"

"I have a lot of extra time on my hands," Freya said. "I thought I should take up a hobby."

"And you chose knitting?"

Freya nodded and said, "Yep. I was at a cafe last week and there were these old ladies there in a group and they all had their knitting out going hell for leather and chatting. It looked like fun."

"So you started knitting?"

"I just went over and asked if they could show me how. They gave me some old needles and a couple of bits of wool and voila! I started a scarf. Only cost me a round of flat whites too," Freya said, smiling.

"Good for you," Maddie said.

"And the best part is because I have something to do with my hands, I've stopped biting my nails. See?" Freya showed Maddie her fingernails.

"Wow," Maddie said. Freya had been a chronic nail-biter for as long she'd known her.

"Oh," Freya said. "I almost forgot. I've been writing again too. It's amazing how knitting frees up your mind."

"Wow. Really?"

Freya shrugged. "Yeah. Most of it's crap, but at least it's crap I can work with right?" Before Maddie could reply, Freya asked, "So, what have you been up to on your break?"

"I've just been hanging out, really."

"With who? Jo? She doesn't seem like the hanging out type," Freya said. "She's not there is she?"

Maddie laughed. "No, she's not. I've met some of the locals and we've been hanging out."

"I'm not sure how I feel about you having fun without me."

"You wouldn't like it. The town's way too small for your ego," Maddie teased.

"Haha," Freya said. "So where is this small town? Or is that a secret?"

"I'm in Chesterfield," Maddie said. "You won't have heard of it. I hadn't."

"Chesterfield, Chesterfield...," Freya said leaning into the camera.

"What are you doing?"

"I'm googling it. Hang on." Freya squinted at the screen and screwed up her nose in concentration.

"Seriously?"

"Here it is. Chesterfield. Heart of the sugar cane industry. Blah, blah some famous person I've never heard of, population..." Freya whistled. "Population three thousand. Wow, you weren't kidding when you said you wanted to get away from people."

"Like I said, it was Jo's idea."

"Yeah, right. So what's it like being in a small town?"

"It's quiet," Maddie said. "And it's nice."

"You're not exactly selling it to me," Freya said. "What's to do in Chesterfield?"

"It's a small town, so not much. It's mostly farms out where I'm staying."

"Right," Freya said, obviously unimpressed.

"I won an ice cream in a belly flop competition," Maddie said.

"Ooh, exciting. Tell me more."

Maddie knew Freya was being sarcastic but she decided to tell her the story anyway. "Tess and I did a tandem dive and won the judge's choice."

"Wait a minute, wait a minute. Who's Tess?"

"Oh, she's a girl I've met," Maddie said. "We've been hanging out."

"Hanging out?"

"Yeah," Maddie said. "I've been helping out with a festival they were meant to be having on the weekend."

"What sort of festival?" Freya asked.

"I think it's kind of like a fete. You know like we used to have in primary school?"

"So, like, kiddies rides and a dunk tank and stuff?"

Maddie shrugged. "I'm not too sure, actually, but there's a lot of baking involved. They had some local bands playing too. They were supposed to burn a block of cane to close it out but it burned last night, so that's not going to happen now, and they're not even sure if it will go ahead."

"Bummer," Freya said. "I've never seen a cane fire."

"They're pretty spectacular," Maddie said, remembering the fire from last night. Which reminded her about helping out with Tess's supposed intervention. "Hey, sorry to cut this short, but I have to get going. I've got a few things I need to do."

"Would these things have anything to do with Tess?" Freya asked.

"Maybe," Maddie said. "But we're just friends."

"Are you sure that's all it is?" Freya asked. She moved closer to the camera so she was just an eyeball looking straight at Maddie.

Maddie laughed. "Go away! There's nothing to tell I promise."

Freya moved back from the camera and said, "You'd tell me though, right? I need to know who I'm competing with for your attention."

"You'll be the first to know," Maddie promised. "Tell Andy I said hi. And I'll let you know when I'm coming back. It'll be soon, I promise."

"Okay. I'm not sure if we'll be able to get him away from his surfboard if he has too much more time with it."

Maddie laughed. "We'll talk soon, okay?"

"Okay."

"And keep knitting. I want to see that scarf finished when I get back."

Freya saluted and said, "Yes boss."

Maddie laughed. "Bye."

"Bye!" Freya was gone.

Maddie shut down the laptop and checked her watch. If she hurried, she might be able to get to the bakery to grab some sweets for later.

Eighteen

"DO YOU THINK HE'LL go for it?" Lizzie asked Will as they strode across the yard to the sheds.

"Not sure, but it's worth a try. Are you sure we shouldn't tell Tess what we're doing?"

"Positive," said Lizzie. "You heard her yesterday. She doesn't want the festival to change."

"But the fire last night might have made her change her mind."

"I don't think so. She's been moping all morning about it. I think we just talk to Pop and see what he says."

"Whatever you say," Will said. "But I think she's going to be pretty upset when she finds out we went behind her back."

"She'll only be upset for a little while. Especially if we pull it off. And don't worry. I'll take all of the blame."

"Whatever," Will said. "Hey, what do you think of Tess and Maddie? They seem to be hitting it off."

"Yeah, they seem to be," Lizzie agreed. "They looked pretty close in that photo you sent me on Monday."

Will shrugged. "That was pretty innocent. Tess was helping Maddie get up to the diving board because of her sore ankle."

"Right," Lizzie said. "So why did you send it through to me then?"

"I thought they looked cute together." Will laughed when Lizzie gave him a friendly shove.

"Is that why you've set them up on a date?" Lizzie asked.

Will put his hand to his chest. "Me? Set Tess up?"

"I know you Will Armstrong, and I know what you're up to."

Will shrugged. "It's pretty obvious they like each other, and after the fire last night, there's no way Tess was going to do anything about it. Besides, she needs to get out of the house and have some fun."

"Yeah, well I hope it doesn't backfire," Lizzie said.

As they rounded the corner of the shed, they could hear raised voices coming from inside. They slowed down to listen.

"If I find out you were behind it, there'll be hell to pay."

"Pop," Will mouthed to Lizzie and then turned his attention back to the shed.

"Now Jack, why on earth would I, or anyone else for that matter, deliberately burn your cane? The question is, what's going to happen to the festival now? That's what I want to know."

Lizzie dug Will in the ribs and when he turned around she whispered, "Barry Montgomery." Will nodded. Barry Montgomery was the Deputy Mayor and an all-round sleaze. As soon as he'd been elected to council a few years ago, he'd changed the planning laws to allow him to redevelop his farm, and instead of people being angry with him, he just threw money at every organisation he could find so they couldn't say a bad word about it. Pop was one of the only people not to accept Barry's money, but the grants from the council he got every year helped pay some of the costs for the festival. If Barry took that away, who knew how they'd cover the extra costs.

"You're not getting it, that's for sure," Pop said. "The festival's a Copeland tradition, and as long as I'm alive, it's going to stay that way."

"Well, I don't think the council can keep supporting it. Especially considering it's not bringing in the tourists it used to."

"So you're not giving anything at all?"

"We can't. Budget's tight. You know that."

"Not tight enough to stop you and Mack Ferguson from going to China next year."

"That's a trade trip," Barry said. "Very important for our agriculture."

There was a bang. "So you want to take the festival by stealth? We fail, and then you can swoop in with funding you just happen to have hiding away somewhere that didn't exist when we needed it? It's not bloody happening."

Before Will could stop her, Lizzie strode past him into the shed. He had no choice but to follow.

"Hi, Pop," Lizzie said as if everything was rosy and she hadn't heard any of the conversation. "I just wanted to make sure it was still okay for us to come take some photos tomorrow?"

Pop looked at Will, who shrugged. Pop said, "Tomorrow?"

"I know it was meant to be today, but those new bands we organised aren't going to be here until the morning, and we'd really like to get a few shots of them setting up."

"The new bands?" Pop said.

"Yeah," Will chimed in. "The ones we spoke about last night."

Pop narrowed his eyes and Will was sure he was going to remind him of the answer he gave last night but instead he said, "Sure. Tomorrow's fine."

"Great," Lizzie said. "Dad's holding the front page for you this year, so we'll do a big feature. He's even talking about doing a double-page spread next week with photos and stories from people who came." She turned her charms on Barry. "I'd love to know how much the council is giving this year to help with expenses, Mr

Montgomery," she said. "So we can include it in the article."

"Oh, er, I'm not sure we're able to help out this year," he said, looking from Lizzie, to Pop, and back again.

"That's a shame," Lizzie said. "Isn't it a shame, Will?"

"A real shame," Will agreed.

Lizzie continued. "I mean, the election's at the end of next year and it would be great to do a story on how much Mr Montgomery and the council gave to the only major music festival in Chesterfield to keep it going."

"Music festival?" Barry asked.

Lizzie nodded enthusiastically. "Yes. Pop's been thinking about changing the festival up for a few years now, and this year, well, he just felt like it was the right time to take advantage of the younger crowd. Right, Will?"

"Right," Will said. He looked at Pop, who still appeared to be in shock.

"You have no idea how many people have been contacting me asking me for details this year," Lizzie said. "It's going to be huge. So anyway, it would be great if you could come back tomorrow so we can take a photo of you handing the cheque to Pop. It would make a great front-page story, don't you think?"

"Well, I—"

"We can sort it all out tomorrow," Lizzie said, smiling sweetly at Barry and then at Pop.

Barry smoothed down what little hair he had left on his head and said, "Right then. I guess I'll see you tomorrow." He walked out into the yard and disappeared around the corner.

Lizzie turned to Will and smiled and then turned to Pop who said, very quietly, "You two better have a bloody good explanation for what just happened."

"I can't believe he's letting us run with it," Will said. He crossed off the name of a band on his long list that had said they couldn't make it to the festival.

"I know," Lizzie said. She changed the background picture on the screen and said, "How about that?"

"I liked the other one," Will said, peering over Lizzie's shoulder. "I really hope we can get it organised in time."

"No sweat," Lizzie replied. "Which other one? I've shown you, like, ten different ones."

"The blue one. With the lights."

Lizzie flicked through the gallery and brought up a picture. "This one?"

"Yeah, that's it."

"Or this one?" Lizzie said, switching to the next picture.

Will peered at it and sighed. "I have no idea. I feel like my brain's going to explode. Just pick one, Lizzie. It's not like it's for real."

"Yeah but we have to treat it like it is, otherwise she won't get the full effect."

"I think she'll get it. When are we going to tell her anyway?"

"Not until Saturday morning," Lizzie said, replacing the red background with a dark blue one. She systematically changed all the text boxes on the mock-up poster on the screen to make the words easier to read and then sat back and admired her work. "I think that's it," she said, crossing her arms over her chest.

"I like it," Will said.

"I'll email this to dad and get him to print it out on the work printer. How many more bands have you got to hear back from?" Lizzie said as she opened an explorer window.

"Just two I think." Will consulted his notebook. "Yeah, two. Just Anchor and Double Cross to go."

"How many is that now?"

"Eight. That's almost a fifty percent hit rate. Not bad for short notice."

Lizzie nodded and started tapping on her keyboard. "We've started getting some followers on Twitter already. Obviously, we'll have heaps more next year."

"If there's a next year."

"There'll be a next year," Lizzie said, posting an update for their followers. "A better website would make a huge difference, but we have to work with what we have. Once we start making some money—"

"If we start making money," Will said.

"When we start making money," Lizzie said, ignoring Will's pessimism. "We'll be able to pay someone to do up a website that we can take bookings for camping and bands and stuff, all in the one place. That'll make things so much easier, don't you think?"

"Yeah, whatever," Will said, though he had no idea about websites. Lizzie was the internet and social media nerd, so he found it easier to just agree with whatever she said. His phone rang. "It's the guy from Anchor. Hello?" Lizzie watched him expectantly. "Yep. Free camping and free food. How many are we expecting?" He looked over to Lizzie who gave him nothing. "I'd reckon a couple thousand." Lizzie slapped her forehead and shook her head. Will shrugged. "Yeah, I know. It's going to be huge. Excellent. That's great. We'll see you Saturday arvo then." He hung up.

"A couple thousand?" Lizzie asked. "Are you serious?"

"You were the one who said to aim high," Will said, putting a tick beside Anchor's name on his book.

"Not that high. You shouldn't be promising more than we can deliver."

"We don't know what we can deliver. Besides, isn't that your job? To get people excited about it on social media?"

"Yeah but so far all we have are small bands who have a handful of fans between them. We haven't got a big name act to bring people in."

"Something will come up," Will said.

Lizzie didn't know whether to strangle him or be happy that he'd stopped being so pessimistic. Before she could say anything more, Will's phone rang again and he said, "That'll be the last one. Fingers crossed."

Nineteen

TESS THUMBED THROUGH THE messages on her phone. There were three from Maddie, five from Lizzie, and one from Will. They all asked if she was up for hanging out (she wasn't), how she was doing after last night (crap), or telling her to call them if she wanted to talk (she didn't). She chewed on the corner of her thumbnail and considered texting Maddie to see how her appointment went this morning. She decided against it because as soon as she sent Maddie a text, she'd probably assume Tess wanted to talk. She tossed her phone onto the bed beside her. She closed her eyes, lay back on her pillow and sighed.

She'd been waiting all day to talk to Pop but he'd been holed up in the sheds doing who-knew-what, so she hadn't even seen him. She'd thought about just going down to the sheds and confronting him, but the way she figured it, the longer he had to cool down and think about the festival without her interfering, the higher the chances he'd decide not to cancel it. At the moment, those chances were still pretty slim, and the fact that Gran hadn't done any more baking told Tess all she needed to know about the current fate of the Crush Festival.

Tess was considering her chances of sneaking out for a snack without running into Gran when she was startled by a knocking on her window. She sat up and pulled back the curtain. Standing on the other side, grinning, was Maddie. Tess pushed out the window and asked, "What are you doing?"

"I was just wondering if you wanted to come to dinner," Maddie said.

"Why didn't you come to the door like a normal person?"

"Because normal's boring. Anyway, I thought it might be a bit more romantic doing it like this."

"Romantic?"

"Yeah. You know, like Romeo and Juliet sneaking out at night."

"Right," Tess said. "So you'd be Romeo then?"

"At your service, my fair Juliet," Maddie said and bowed low.

Tess smiled in spite of herself and shook her head. She leaned out the window and looked around, expecting to see Will and Lizzie hiding somewhere nearby.

"It's just me," Maddie said, answering the question Tess hadn't asked. "No-one knows I'm here. Are you coming or not?"

"I don't really feel like talking," Tess said.

"You don't have to talk. It's just dinner, Tess. I've already told Gran you won't be here tonight, so if you don't come you'll be fending for yourself."

Tess sighed. What harm could it do to get out of the house anyway? She'd only be wallowing like she'd done all day, and spending time with Maddie would be a good distraction. "Fine," she said. "I'll meet you around the back."

"Can't you just climb out the window?" Maddie asked.

"I haven't climbed out of this window in years."

"Live dangerously for a while," Maddie said. "Pretend you've been kept against your will and you're finally able to escape with the help of your knight in shining armour."

Tess laughed in spite of herself. She said, "You know I turn into a pumpkin after midnight?"

"I'll have you home well before then, Cinderella," Maddie said.

"I thought I was Juliet?" Tess said.

"You can be whoever you like, Princess," Maddie replied, grinning.

Tess climbed up onto the window sill and swung her legs out. She pushed the window out to give her some more room, and then pushed herself off, landing on the grass in a crouch.

"That drop always looked so much bigger when I was little." She dusted herself off.

"Where are you taking me?"

Maddie took Tess's hand. "You'll see."

Tess's suspicions that Will and Lizzie were involved were confirmed when Maddie took Tess up to the treehouse on Chitty. Tess had warned Maddie that Chitty could be cantankerous when they'd come up to swim in the dam, but Maddie had obviously been shown how to start it by someone. Plus, the treehouse was cleaner than it had been in a long time, and Maddie had put out little LED candles around inside to give them some light. The sun hadn't gone down yet, but even with the window open all the way, inside was dark because of the shadows from the trees on the side of the dam.

Maddie spread plastic containers out onto a blanket and popped open the lids on each one.

"This looks fantastic," Tess said. She settled herself on the floor and pulled her legs underneath her.

"Will and Lizzie gave me a hand to set it all up," Maddie said.

"I knew it," Tess replied.

"We all wanted you to get out of the house for a while," Maddie said, pouring orange juice into two plastic cups. She handed one to Tess and said, "We should toast to something."

"Like what?" Tess asked, taking her cup.

"I don't know. How about... oh, how about to not getting killed on Sunday?"

"Why would you toast that? You hurt your ankle."

"Yeah, but I also met you." Maddie cocked her head to the side and smiled.

Tess smiled back. "To not getting killed on Sunday then," she said. She clinked cups with Maddie and they each took a sip.

"Do you want to talk about what happened with the fire?" Maddie asked.

"Not really," Tess replied. "Thanks for getting me out of the house though."

"That's okay," Maddie said. "If you'd said no to me asking you on a date, Will and Lizzie were going to come and kidnap you and take you to Lizzie's house."

Tess laughed. "Really?"

"Yeah," Maddie nodded. She took a strawberry from a plate, dipped it into a pot of cream, pointed it at Tess and said, "Lucky for you, they both had stuff on tonight." She took a bite of the strawberry and dropped the green tip back into the container.

"What kind of stuff?" Tess asked. She peered into the food containers and decided on biscuits and cheese.

"Lizzie had to work and Will had band practice."

Tess nodded. Just like them to figure that the festival would still be going ahead. She pulled out a piece of coconut ice from a container and said, "Is this Gran's?"

Maddie nodded. "She said she had some spare since the festival might not happen now."

Tess put the sweet back into the container and wiped her fingers on a paper napkin.

"Sorry," Maddie said. She looked around the treehouse. "You must've had some great times in this place."

"The secrets this place could tell if it could talk," Tess said, glad for the change of subject.

"Like what?"

"Little kid stuff mostly. We formed two secret clubs up here when we were in primary school. And whatever was said in the treehouse stayed in the treehouse."

"Secret societies, huh?"

"Yeah, among other things."

"Such as?"

"Such as, Will and Lizzie had their first kiss up here."

"Huh," Maddie said. "Will and Lizzie don't act like a couple."

"That's because they also broke up here."

"Oh. That's sad."

"Not really. They're much better as friends."

Maddie knew exactly what Tess was talking about. "What about you?" she asked.

"What about me?"

"What deep, dark secret have you told the treehouse?"

Tess replied, "This is where I came out to Lizzie and Will."

"That's pretty huge." Maddie pulled a wrapper from a chocolate and took a bite.

Tess smiled and said, "Yeah. It wasn't a big deal though. I was never really in if you know what I mean."

"Yeah," Maddie said absently. She took a sip of her drink and balled up the chocolate wrapper in her hand. "It feels like that sort of place, doesn't it?" she said finally.

"What do you mean?"

"The sort of place you could say anything and not worry about the consequences."

Tess had never really thought about the treehouse like that before. Probably because it had always been that sort of place for her. A place that felt like it was a million miles away from the rest of the world. "I guess so," she said.

Maddie didn't reply, so they sat in silence for a while, listening to tree branches scraping against the sides of the treehouse. Then Maddie said, "Can I add a secret of my own?"

"I guess so," Tess said.

"The treehouse rules apply?" Maddie asked. "Whatever is said here, stays here?"

"Of course."

Maddie took a deep breath and let it out slowly. She turned to Tess and said, "I'm going to tell you something Tess, and it's a huge secret."

"Okay."

"And I don't want you to freak out on me." The way Maddie looked at Tess, it was like she was afraid that whatever she was about to say, it might make Tess run for the hills.

"Okay," Tess said.

Maddie chewed on her cup and said, "It's stupid."

Tess laughed, and said, "You have no idea how many stupid things this treehouse has heard. It can't possibly be any worse."

Maddie smiled and said, "It's not stupid as in it's a silly thing. I mean it's stupid that I'm finding it so hard to tell you."

"Wow," Tess said. "It must be huge. Don't tell me then. Let me guess." She tapped her chin. "I know. You're on the run from the law."

Maddie laughed. "No."

"Hmm, what else could it be?" Tess bit into a biscuit and chewed slowly. "Are you a spy on a secret assignment?"

"In a place like Chesterfield?" Maddie asked.

"Good point," Tess conceded. "The only controversial thing going on out here is Gary Evans wanting to plow in his cane and plant macadamias."

"Really? People are worried about that?"

"You have no idea," Tess said. "Hmm, what else could it be?" She looked at Maddie, who seemed to be enjoying the game. "Oh my God, I know what it is."

"What?" Maddie asked.

"You," Tess said, pointing at Maddie, "are a famous actress in some sort of trouble who's trying to avoid the spotlight."

The colour drained from Maddie's face and she swallowed hard.

"What?" Tess asked. "What's wrong?" She felt like she'd touched a nerve.

Maddie took several deep breaths. "Okay," she said finally. "I'm going to have to tell you." She looked into Tess's eyes. Tess felt herself leaning forward, and thought she might burst from the anticipation. Maddie's phone rang, breaking the tension, making them both laugh. Maddie looked at the screen and said, "It's Jo. I should answer it." Maddie swiped the screen and said, "Hello, Jo. I'm kind of in the middle of something. Can I call you back?" She looked up at Tess and gave her a little smile. Then her face dropped and she stood up and walked to the door of the treehouse, turning her back on Tess. She lowered her voice and Tess couldn't quite make out what Maddie was saying.

After a few seconds of muffled talking, Maddie raised her voice. "I don't care. I'm not going back," she said. Then her shoulders slumped and she said, "Fine. I'll be there soon." She hung up and turned back to Tess. "I'm so sorry. I've got something I need to sort out. Can we take a rain check?"

"Sure. I guess," Tess said. She started putting lids back on food containers. "What about tomorrow?"

"Tomorrow's good," Maddie said, kneeling down to help Tess pack up. "Lunch?"

Tess nodded. "What if we go into town? There's a really great takeaway place called Piggies'. They make the best burgers and chips in town."

Maddie smiled and said, "Sounds great. I can meet you there? Say around one o'clock?"

"Great," Tess said. "Oh, I almost forgot. Lizzie's having a movie night tomorrow night. I was going over around three. Did you want to come?"

"Sure," Maddie said.

"I'll be staying at Lizzie's for the night so it's okay if you can't, you know if Jo wants you home."

Maddie smiled and said, "I'll ask Jo. She should be able to look after herself for one night."

Twenty

TESS SAT ON THE bench outside Piggies' waiting for Maddie. She wasn't as nervous as she thought she'd be. She guessed that was because technically, even though it was interrupted, they'd had their first official date last night. Plus she was also more than a little curious about the so-called 'big secret' Maddie didn't get the chance to tell her and wondered if it had anything to do with Jo.

"Hey," Maddie called. Tess looked up to see her walking along the footpath. She was wearing a summer dress that floated around her knees as she walked, a plain red baseball cap pulled down on her head and a backpack slung over one shoulder. Tess felt a little underdressed in her cargo shorts and t-shirt.

Tess stood up and Maddie greeted her with a hug.

"What's in the bag?" Tess asked.

"Spare clothes and stuff. For staying at Lizzie's tonight."

"Oh."

"Aren't we staying at Lizzie's tonight?" Maddie asked, looking confused.

"Yes, we are. I just didn't know whether Jo would let you stay out."

"Pfft," Maddie said, waving her hand like she was swatting a fly. "Jo's a pushover."

"Okay then," Tess smiled. Her stomach fluttered at the thought of spending the night with Maddie. She opened the door to Piggies' and ushered Maddie inside. The heat from the fryers hit them as they walked over to the counter, and it was just starting to get busy with the lunch rush.

Mrs Hemingway, the owner of Piggies' and one of Gran's oldest friends, greeted them and said, "I heard about the fire. Hope no-one was hurt?" She wiped her hands on her apron and pulled a pen from behind her ear.

"Everyone's fine," Tess said. "The cane paddock's trashed though."

"Shame," Mrs Hemingway said. "What can I get you, girls?"

Maddie leaned into Tess and asked, "What do you think?"

"The chicken burger is one of the best you'll ever have," Tess replied. "Unless, you know, you want a salad or something."

"A chicken burger is fine," Maddie said, giving Tess a nudge with her shoulder.

"Two chicken burgers," Mrs Hemingway said. "Chips?"

Tess glanced at Maddie who said, "We can share some?"

Mrs Hemingway nodded. "Chips for two. Any drinks?"

"Lime milkshake for me, thanks," Tess said.

"Make that two," Maddie said.

Mrs Hemingway shook her head and said, "Now I know two crazy people who drink green milk." She rang up the order and Tess paid, despite Maddie insisting on paying for her half. As she took Tess's money, Mrs Hemingway asked, "Do either of you girls know someone called India?"

Tess shook her head. "No. Why?"

"A young man, about your age, came in yesterday afternoon looking for someone called India something-or-other. Something like that. Said he was a friend of hers and thought she might be staying around here somewhere. I thought you might've known her from school or something."

"Not me," Tess said, though she thought there might be something vaguely familiar about the name. "Maddie?" Tess asked.

"No," Maddie said. "No-one I know."

Tess thought Maddie had gone a little bit green. "Are you feeling okay? You look a little sick."

"I'm okay," Maddie said.

Tess led Maddie over to a table in the corner to wait for their order. "Are you sure you're okay?"

Maddie nodded. "I'm fine. It's just really hot in here." She fanned herself with a menu. Though she couldn't be sure, she had a funny feeling that the man may have been asking about her. Could her father have hired someone to track her down? She certainly wouldn't put it past him. She didn't want to think about it so she asked Tess, "Is the festival still cancelled?"

"I haven't seen Pop much, so I don't know. Gran's okay I guess."

"What about you?"

Tess shrugged. "I'm okay. I just don't know what I'm going to do if Pop doesn't change his mind."

Maddie took Tess's hand and said, "I'm sorry, Tess. I'm sure we'll come up with something."

"I hope so."

Mrs Hemingway brought out their lunch and Maddie said, "Can we go somewhere where there's not so many people?"?

Chesterfield wasn't exactly a buzzing city, but Tess guessed that Maddie just wanted some privacy, so she led her across to the show grounds. The gates were always locked but there was a hole in the fence that had been there forever that backed onto the horse stables.

Tess held up the wire fence for Maddie to duck under, handed her the lunch bags, and ducked under herself. She took Maddie's hand and lead her past the stables and around to the old grandstand. They climbed right up to the last row of seats and sat down. Tess unfolded the newspaper covering the chips and spread it out between them. Maddie bit into her burger and laughed when mayonnaise dripped down her chin.

"Good?" Tess asked, biting into her own burger.

Maddie nodded. They sat and ate in silence and when Maddie had finished her burger, she leaned back on the seat and said, "I'm so full."

Tess licked the mayonnaise and salt from her fingers and wiped her hand on a napkin.

"What's the plan when we get to Lizzie's?" Maddie asked.

"Movies I think. And most likely karaoke. Lizzie loves karaoke."

"You don't?"

Tess shrugged. "Not really. I'm pretty much tone deaf so it's not my thing."

"You don't like music?" Maddie asked.

"I like music. Just not as much as Will and Lizzie do." Tess thought she'd disappointed Maddie with her answer, but wasn't exactly sure why. "What about you?" she asked. "Do you like music?" Tess stuffed the last of the chips into her mouth and took a long drink of her milkshake. Maddie looked out at the show ring and sighed. For some reason Tess couldn't put her finger on, she felt like she'd hit a nerve.

Maddie brushed her hands off on her dress and said, "So you know that thing I was going to tell you at the treehouse?"

"Your big secret?" Tess teased.

Maddie smiled and said, "Yeah." She took Tess's hand and said, "If I tell you, you have to promise not to freak out."

"Okay."

Maddie took a deep breath and closed her eyes. When she opened them she said, "I'm Indiana Rose."

She looked at Tess intently. Tess looked back at her, waiting for more information. When Maddie didn't say anything more, Tess said, "You know I really have no idea what you're talking about."

"You know Lizzie's favourite band? Three's Company?"

It hit Tess all of a sudden where she'd heard that name before. "Holy shit," she said. "Holy shit. You're Lizzie's favourite band?"

"Part of," Maddie said.

"But, Lizzie said she'd, I mean you'd gone to rehab."

"Do I look like I'm in rehab?" Maddie asked.

Tess laughed at the absurdity of it. "Of course not," she said. She shook her head. "Lizzie's going to pee her freaking pants when she finds out."

"No, Tess. You can't tell her."

"But—"

Maddie pulled her hand away and turned away from Tess. "I didn't tell you so you could tell Lizzie."

"Okay. Treehouse rules, remember?" Tess said, taking Maddie's hand back.

"That applies even though we're not in the treehouse?"

"Sure. You were going to tell me last night, so the rules still apply."

Maddie smiled. She seemed relieved.

"Why did you tell me?" Tess asked.

Maddie shrugged. "I don't know. I guess I just... I really like you, Tess and I felt like I've been lying to you about who I am."

"So you're not who I think you are?"

"What do you mean?"

"The jumping off diving boards, running in the middle of the day in white tracksuits, the sweet tooth. That's not really you?"

"Of course it is," Maddie replied.

"Then you haven't been lying to me," Tess said.

Maddie smiled. "Thanks."

"So should I still call you Maddie?" Tess asked.

"Maddie's my real name. Indiana Rose is just a stage name."

"Right. So, you being up here is the reason the concerts were cancelled?"

"Sort of," Maddie said. "It's complicated but the short story is that I had a fight with my dad and I guess I just had enough. I needed a break."

"And you picked Chesterfield because..."

"Jo's family owns the McGregor house."

"So Jo's a McGregor," Tess said. Now it was all starting to come together. Except for one thing. "How do you know Jo?"

"She's my bodyguard," Maddie said like everyone had one.

"No wonder I feel like she's going to shoot me every time she sees me," Tess said.

Maddie laughed. "She can be overprotective, but that's what I pay her for."

"Why isn't she here then? Protecting you from me?"

"You're not a threat, Tess."

"What am I then?" Though Tess was only teasing with the question, she was dying for Maddie to confirm that what they were both feeling was real.

Maddie looked down at the ground and twisted her napkin. She looked sideways at Tess and said quietly, "You're someone I'd like to kiss."

Tess's heart leaped straight into her mouth and she had to remind herself to breathe. Maddie leaned in and Tess moved along the seat closing the gap between them and scrunching the empty chip wrapper. It seemed to take forever, but when their lips met, Tess finally felt like she could breathe again. She felt like the world had stopped, and there was no-one else in it except for her and Maddie. When they broke apart, Maddie said, "You taste like chicken salt."

Tess laughed. "You taste like mayonnaise." She took a long drink of her milkshake and looked out over the centre ring. She knew she should still be feeling bad about the fire and the state of the festival, but Maddie's kiss had just wiped all of that away. At least for the moment, and it was hard to see how today could get any better.

Twenty-One

LIZZIE'S GAMES ROOM WAS a testament to her older brother Lee, who'd bought every high-tech gadget known to man thanks to working at Michael's Electronics before he went overseas three years ago. A massive flat-screen TV took up one wall and below it sat a cabinet with games consoles and games dating back to the 1980s. Tess wasn't sure if some of the older ones even worked but Lee collected them like some people collected stamps.

Lizzie's pride and joy though was her karaoke machine. Tess and Maddie hadn't been at Lizzie's for more than an hour when Lizzie started hooking it up to the TV. Tess groaned.

"Oh come on, Tess. You knew this was what we'd be doing today."

"I thought you'd at least let Maddie get settled before subjecting her to karaoke," Tess said.

Lizzie pulled a face and continued connecting and disconnecting cords and microphones.

"Well, I'm going to get another drink and refill the chips," Tess said. "Do you want to give me a hand, Maddie?" Tess gave her the 'you need to come with me now' look and thankfully, Maddie got the hint and followed Tess out into the hall.

When they got to the kitchen, and far enough away that Tess thought Lizzie wouldn't be able to hear them, she said, "You don't have to sing if you don't want to."

Maddie opened a packet of chips, dumped its contents into the bowl, and said, "I'll be fine."

"Don't you think Lizzie will guess who you are as soon as you start singing? She is your number one fan."

"Give me some credit," Maddie said, crunching on a chip. "I can sing badly when I want to." She winked at Tess, picked up the bowl of chips, kissed Tess on the cheek, and headed back down to the games room.

Maddie certainly wasn't wrong. Lizzie insisted they sing duet battles on some of Maddie's own songs, which Lizzie had made into karaoke versions on her computer, and despite Tess's reservations, Maddie killed them. Really, terribly, killed them. Maddie sang so badly that Lizzie pulled Tess aside after only the third song and whispered, "She's almost as bad as you. I think we should just watch a movie before she destroys any more of my favourite songs."

"I think she's a great singer," Tess said.

Lizzie, obviously missing the sarcasm, said, "You would think that since you're tone-deaf."

The insult didn't bother Tess. She was secretly happy to get out of singing karaoke herself. Lizzie opened the movie cabinet and instructed Tess and Maddie to choose one movie each. Tess's only stipulation was that Lizzie couldn't choose 'The Sound of Music' because there were only so many times she could listen to Lizzie sing 'Do Re Me'. Lizzie picked 'The Rocky Horror Picture Show' instead and, Tess thought, just to spite her. Maddie picked 'The Lion King' and Tess picked 'Footloose'. The original, not the remake.

"We should watch yours first," Tess said to Lizzie. "Just to get the singing out of your system." Lizzie poked her tongue out and put the DVD into the player. Tess and Maddie settled down side-by-side on the lounge. It was thrilling for Tess to be snuggling so close with Maddie, even though Lizzie was in the same room. It was even better when Lizzie closed the blockout curtains to make the room dark to stop the glare on the TV screen. Maddie curled her legs up beside her, slipped her hand into Tess's, and leaned her head on Tess's shoulder. Tess was hyper-aware of every part of her skin that Maddie touched and found it hard to concentrate on the movie. It didn't matter. She knew it off by heart, thanks to Lizzie's obsession with musicals.

After a three-movie marathon, and even though it was late, Lizzie insisted on watching one of Lee's D-grade horror movies before they went to sleep. They were about two-thirds through the movie when Will came in. It must have been almost midnight, so Tess was surprised to see him.

"What are you doing here so late?" Tess asked as Will took a handful of chips and plopped down on a beanbag beside Lizzie.

"I was bored," he said like he did this sort of thing all the time. "What are we watching?"

"Murder in Scarlet," Lizzie said.

"Ooh, have you gotten to the part yet where we find out the secret of the murderer?"

Lizzie whacked Will on the arm and said, "Shh, Maddie hasn't seen it."

"Sorry," Will said and stuffed more chips into his mouth.

"Where have you been?" Tess asked.

"Messing around with the band. And talking to—Ow!" Lizzie had punched him hard on the arm.

"Talking to who?" Tess asked.

"No-one," Lizzie said at the same time Will said, "People."

Something was going on, Tess thought, and she didn't like it. "What's going on? Lizzie?"

"Watch the movie," Lizzie said.

"You've seen it a hundred times," Tess said.

"Maddie hasn't," Lizzie replied.

"I don't mind," Maddie said. "Your conversation sounds much more interesting."

Tess paused the movie just as the main character walked in on one of the killers. It was a pivotal moment in the movie and Lizzie said, "It's just getting to the good part."

"Spill," Tess said to Will.

Lizzie shook her head and said, "Not until Saturday."

"Why not now?"

"Because nothing's been finalised yet," Will said.

"What hasn't been finalised?"

Will opened his mouth to say something but Lizzie was quick and covered his mouth with her hand. "It's a surprise."

"I hate surprises," Tess said.

"Do you?" Maddie asked.

"No. She doesn't," Lizzie said. "She loves surprises. She just hates finding out about them beforehand. Which is why we're not telling you until Saturday."

Tess glared at Will and Lizzie but they just looked at her innocently. "Fine," Tess said and pressed play on the movie. The main character screamed when the real killer turned around, holding her red-haired wig in her hand revealing that she wasn't really a red-head in the first place. They all jumped when someone's phone rang at the exact same moment.

"Sorry," Maddie said, digging her phone out of her bag. She swiped the front of her phone and said, "It's Jo." Tess looked back to the TV, not wanting to spy on Maddie's text messages. She wondered whether Jo had a tracker that told her when Maddie was having too much fun so she could spoil it. Maddie sat up and said, "Oh no."

"What?" Tess sat up too.

"I have to go," Maddie said.

"Now?"

"But the movie's nearly finished. Can't you wait until the end?"

"Apparently not," Maddie said. "That thing I told you about today?" she said to Tess. Tess nodded. "I have to go sort it out. Jo said she's out front waiting."

Tess stood up and helped Maddie collect her things. "I'll walk you out."

"Thanks for having me, Lizzie," Maddie said, tossing her backpack over her shoulder. "I've had a great time. And I loved karaoke."

"Any time," Lizzie replied.

Tess walked Maddie to the front door and before she opened it, she pulled Maddie into a hug.

"Thanks for today," Maddie said. "You've made me feel like a normal person."

"And you made me forget about the festival. At least for a couple of hours," Tess replied.

"I'm sorry I have to go. I really wanted to stay tonight," Maddie said. She leaned in and kissed

Tess on the lips. It was soft and sweet and promised more to come. When they broke apart, Maddie leaned her forehead on Tess's.

"Is everything okay?" Tess asked.

"I hope so," Maddie replied.

"I'll see you tomorrow?"

Maddie paused and then said, "Yeah."

Tess opened the door and sure enough, Jo's car was waiting in the driveway. Maddie kissed Tess on the cheek and said, "Bye."

"Bye," Tess said. She waited until the car pulled away before she closed the door. She took a few deep breaths and then headed back to Lizzie and Will.

"I worked out who Maddie looks like," Will said when Tess returned.

"Who?" Tess asked. She plopped down onto the lounge.

"He's got no idea," Lizzie said.

"That lead singer from Three's Company," Will said. "Don't you think?"

Tess's breath caught in her throat. "No idea," she said.

"Her hair is too short and too dark," Lizzie said.

"What do you think, Tess?" Will asked.

Tess took a handful of chips, shoved them into her mouth, and just shrugged.

"Well, she can't sing to save herself," Lizzie said. "And besides, don't you think I'd know if Indiana Rose was in town?"

"I didn't say she was her. I said she looks like her. Kind of."

"You have no idea," Lizzie said. "But speaking of Maddie, you know she was snuggling up pretty close with Tess before?"

Tess almost choked on her chips.

"Really?" Will said. He sat up on the beanbag and said, "Anything you want to tell us?"

"No," Tess said.

"Oh come on," Lizzie said. "Anyone could see you two are together."

"We're not together," Tess said, though she wasn't exactly sure what they were.

"Ooh, Tess and Maddie sitting in a tree," Will sang.

Tess threw a cushion at him and he laughed. "It's cool," he said. "And Maddie's cool too so, you know..."

"It's cool?" Tess said.

Will nodded. "It's cool, right Lizzie?"

"It's cool," Lizzie said.

"Just play the movie," Tess said.

Lizzie pressed play on the movie and Tess was relieved that the conversation was over. Lizzie would kill her if she found out what Tess knew about Maddie, but she didn't want to think about it. She was glad though that Will and Lizzie were happy for her and Maddie, whatever it was they were.

Twenty-two

TESS WAS WOKEN EARLY on Friday morning by Lizzie shaking her, yelling at her to wake up. She rolled over onto her back and stretched.

"What's going on?" Tess asked.

Lizzie shoved her and said, "I can't believe you."

"Can't believe me what?" Tess yawned and opened her eyes.

Lizzie threw a newspaper at her, crossed her arms and said, "I thought we were friends, Tess."

Tess picked up the paper and opened it. She had to blink the sleep out of her eyes, and when she saw the front page, her heart dropped into her stomach. There, taking up most of the page, was a grainy picture of Tess and Maddie sitting in the grandstand at the show grounds, kissing. The headline said 'Starlet Shuns Concerts for Small Town Fling.'

"Oh my God." Tess kicked off the sheets and jumped up. She searched for her phone, found it under her shorts on the floor and cycled through to Maddie's number and dialled. It rang out, and she tried again. No answer. Maddie didn't even have a voice mail so Tess could leave a message. Tess dialled her own voice mail but Maddie hadn't left a message.

"Here I am telling you she reminds me of someone, and you knew all along who she was," Lizzie said, pacing across the room. "And Will. Will actually picked it. He knew she looked like Indiana Rose and you pretended like you didn't know what he was talking about."

Tess checked the time on her phone. 7.30 am. Pop wouldn't be in town for another hour at least, and Tess had to get back to the farm. Now. She text Will to ask if he could take her out earlier, and was elated when he said he could.

"And my Twitter feed," Lizzie continued. "You have no idea. It's just gone nuts! How do you think I feel being the last to know that Indiana-freaking-Rose is in my home town?"

"Lizzie, I didn't know," Tess said, pulling on her shorts.

"How could you not?" Lizzie said. "Look at her!" She shook the paper in front of Tess's face.

Tess snatched it from her and said, "She told me yesterday, okay? I had no idea until she told me yesterday."

"And you still didn't say anything. Tess, you know she's practically my favourite band."

"She made me promise not to tell anyone."

"I'm not just anyone. I'm your best friend. How could you not tell me?" Lizzie's voice was getting shrill. "If that's not betrayal, I don't know what is."

"Betrayal? Don't you think whoever took those pictures is the one who's guilty of betrayal?"

"Are you accusing me?" Lizzie asked.

Tess scoffed. "Of course not, but someone had to know who she was. And your dad was the one who put it on the front page."

"So it's his fault now?"

Tess rolled her eyes.

Lizzie continued. "He didn't have to do anything for your stupid festival you know. He loses money because he can't sell advertising on the same page as the feature because no-one wants to be associated with it."

"What are you talking about?" Tess looked around to make sure she had everything.

"What do you think sells more papers? A story about a stupid festival no-one cares about? Or Indiana Rose on the front page kissing her girlfriend?"

"I'm not her girlfriend," Tess said. At least, she didn't think she was.

"Well at least I know who my true friends are," Lizzie said. "Or in this case, aren't. True friends don't keep secrets like that."

Lizzie turned to walk away but Tess had heard enough. She grabbed Lizzie's arm, spun her around and yelled at her. "Why do you think she was here?"

"I don't know," Lizzie yelled back.

"She was trying to have a break from this," Tess said, shaking the paper in front of Lizzie. "From all this crap. She hates it and she was trying to just..." Tess paused. "To feel normal," she said. "She just wanted to feel normal."

Lizzie pulled her arm away and shrunk back. Tess felt bad about the way she'd spoken to Lizzie but she didn't know what else to do.

"I didn't realise," Lizzie mumbled.

"No," Tess said. "You never do." As soon as the words were out of her mouth and she saw how offended Lizzie was, she regretted them. "I'm sorry," she said.

Lizzie turned away in a huff.

Tess sighed. "Look, I wanted to tell you, but Maddie asked me not to."

Lizzie crossed her arms but still didn't turn around.

Tess tried a different tack. "Lizzie, I really like Maddie. I mean, really, really like her. Like you really liked Will once."

Lizzie turned around, her eyes wide. "Really?"

Tess nodded.

Lizzie sighed. "I'm sorry," she said. "I didn't mean to make fun of you about it last night."

Tess smiled. "It's okay." She put her bag on the bed and sighed. "Look. I have to get back to the farm and see how Maddie is and whether she's seen this yet. We'll talk about it later, okay?"

Lizzie nodded. "Okay."

Tess gathered up the rest of her stuff and shoved it into her bag. "I'll see you later?"

Lizzie nodded. "I'll see if I can find out who took the photos," she said.

"Thank you." Tess pulled Lizzie into a hug. When she let her go, Lizzie said, "I can't believe she sang so badly yesterday." It made Tess laugh. She raked her hair into a ponytail, picked up her bag and headed outside to wait for Will.

Will took Tess straight to the McGregor house where Tess was gutted to discover that Jo and Maddie had already left. As far as Tess was concerned, that could only mean one thing. That Maddie had seen the paper and had left town to get away from the limelight again. Tess tried calling her but again, Maddie didn't answer. Will steered Tess back to the car and said, "Come on. Let's get to the farm and we'll work out what to do from there."

Will drove into the main driveway but didn't get out. "I have to get back to the band," he said. "Sorry I can't stay."

"The band? For what?"

"We, er, might have a gig tomorrow night since the festival's been cancelled. So we're just, you know, practising some new stuff."

"Right," Tess said.

As she climbed out of the car Will said, "Tess, you know this will all blow over? You'll see. No-one will remember the girl from Chesterfield who kissed the superstar singer."

Tess punched him on the arm. He laughed. "I'm serious though. Everything will be fine."

Tess wasn't so sure. "Thanks for the ride," she said.

"No worries. I might catch you later."

Tess stood in the driveway and watched Will drive away. There were trucks and utes still being unpacked in the Big Yard. Some people obviously hadn't heard the news about the festival being cancelled yet. She considered going across and telling them to pack up and go home, but the last thing she wanted to think about right now was the festival. When she got inside, she went straight to her room and shut the door.

She lay on her bed and thumbed through the texts on her phone, lingering on the photo Will had taken at the pool on Monday night. She opened a new message and typed I saw the paper I'm sorry Please call me.

She pressed send. Then she opened another text and typed I miss u xx.

She put her phone on her bedside table and pulled the pillow over her head.

A few hours of playing games on her phone in her room hadn't improved Tess's mood. Neither had the fact that she still hadn't heard from Maddie, and her texts to both Will and Lizzie had gone unanswered. Tess had gone in search of food around lunchtime but had come back to her bedroom to sulk some more. A soft knock on Tess's door pulled her from her funk. "I'm awake," she called.

The door opened and Gran peered in. "Can I come in?"

"Yeah," Tess said. She sat up and hugged her knees to her chest.

Gran sat on the end of her bed. She put her hands in her lap and took a deep breath. The last time she'd done that, she'd told Tess about her cancer. Tess wondered what bad news she had to tell her this time.

"Everything okay?" Gran asked.

Tess shrugged.

"You've been in here for hours. Don't you think it's time you came out to face the world again?"

Tess didn't answer.

Gran tried again. "Have you heard from Maddie?"

Tess shook her head. She played with the cuff of her shorts and willed herself not to get upset. She knew it was probably stupid to cry over a girl she'd only met a week ago. But they'd had so much fun together and Tess felt like she'd known Maddie her whole life. And not knowing whether

Maddie was upset with her over the photo in the paper just killed her.

"I'm sorry she had to leave," Gran said. She patted Tess's foot.

"Did you see them before they left?"

"Jo returned the keys late last night."

"So they left last night?"

Gran nodded.

"But the picture wasn't in the paper until this morning. How did they—"

"I don't think it was about the paper, Tess," Gran said.

"What then?"

"A family matter was what Jo said. I don't know any more than that."

"Then why won't Maddie return my calls?"

"I don't know, Tess. Maybe she just hasn't had time."

Tess looked out her bedroom window. There were still way too many people out there considering the festival had been cancelled. "Has Pop told everyone the festival's not on?" she asked.

Gran looked out the window. "I guess so. Some of those people are from up north I think, so Pop's probably offered to let them stay overnight since they've driven all the way here."

Tess nodded. It'd be hard to wake up tomorrow morning with the Big Yard empty, instead of full of stallholders and people.

As if Gran had read Tess's thoughts, she said, "You know the festival isn't about the cane or the crushing?"

Tess looked at Gran, confused.

"It was at first, but when you were born, it all changed."

"What do you mean?"

Gran smiled. "I remember the day you were born. Your dad called us at three in the morning to tell us your mum was in labour. I wanted to wait until visiting hours to go and see you, but your Pop, he was having none of it." Gran looked up to the ceiling, as if her memories were up there, playing out like a movie. "He jumped out of bed and ordered me into the car and we drove straight to the hospital. We made it just in time. It was his proudest moment, you know. Holding you for the first time when you were only an hour or so old."

"I have that photo," Tess said. It was in a silver frame on her bedside table at home, and it was one of her favourites.

Gran looked back at Tess and smiled. "I must have gone through three rolls of film taking photos of you and your Pop that first week." She laughed and shook her head. "Every chance he got, he'd bring you out here. He had you on the tractors and the haul out trucks before you could walk, showing you the farm. You were six months old when he sat with you in the back of his ute to watch your first cane fire. You were obsessed with them for ages after that. Couldn't get enough of them. Every time you came out here you wanted him to burn the cane for you."

"I'm not sure what that's got to do with the festival," Tess said.

Gran squeezed Tess's knee. "He reinstated the festival for you, Tess."

Tess sat up straighter. "What do you mean? We've always had the festival."

"Not really. It just started off as a bit of a party for the neighbours and workers. We didn't always have the last cane fire. We just sort of fell into it after we did it a few years in a row. People around here just started turning up to see the last block burned every year, and we thought we should probably feed them since they were coming out to watch us." She sighed. "And then one year, a few years before you were born actually, cane fires were banned because of the fire danger and we just never had another one after that."

"Wow. I thought we only missed a year because of too much rain."

Gran laughed. "That's a porky your Pop tells you. I think he likes the legend of the festival more than the truth of it."

"So why would he cancel it? And why doesn't he want to have it again next year?"

"This year, I guess circumstances changed. The council has been giving him grief over funding for years. And as for next year, well. He thinks that once you're off living in the city you'll just get too busy to come back for it. I guess he doesn't want to be disappointed, so he just decided in his own mind that it would be easier to not have it."

"So that's why he's upset about it." It all made sense now. He'd wanted to make it memorable for Tess because he thought it would be the last one. And now that it was cancelled... "I should go and talk to him," Tess said.

"You'll have to wait until he gets back from in town," Gran said. "But you know, Bessie could probably use some company since she'll probably not be needed tomorrow. Pete won't be back until the morning to pick her up."

"Sure," Tess said. She could do with the distraction.

Twenty-three

IT WASN't that her father was angry with her that upset Maddie the most. It was the fact that at no point during their conversation did he acknowledge that the reasons why she'd left were valid. Jo had driven Maddie all the way back to Brisbane to talk to her father face-to-face because of what their record label was threatening, but her father hadn't even bothered to fly up from Sydney. Maddie had wanted to go straight back to Chesterfield but Jo said she had to sort things out with her father for the sake of the band. Jo was right, as always, so she'd settled on calling him via Skype. It turned out to be just as bad as being in the same room as him. Talking via Skype hadn't stopped him from taking over the conversation, and it hadn't stopped him from trying to manipulate her into telling him where she'd been staying or into doing what he wanted her to do.

The last straw came for Maddie when her father informed her that he'd spoken to her agent and asked him to go ahead and pursue the solo deal. That was the point she'd hung up on him.

Jo stood in the corner frowning. She'd heard every word of the one-way conversation and would probably stand up for Maddie's father like she usually did. 'Devil's advocate' she called it. Maddie wondered when Jo would ever advocate for her.

"That's that then," Jo said.

Maddie shrugged. "I guess so. Can you tell Freya and Andy they can come in now? We should probably talk about what we want to do."

Honestly? She had no idea where to go from here. Her father insisted she could go further by herself than with Freya and Andy, but it was Maddie who'd come late to the band. She couldn't imagine being on stage without them, and loved singing knowing they were there with her. At least, she did in the beginning. Before her father decided to become their manager and started trying to tell them what sort of music they should be singing.

Maddie had no idea until a few weeks ago that her dad had been vetting their music for them, deciding what samples they'd get to listen to when they were putting their last album together. Some of the songs were okay, sure, but most of them weren't meant for bands like

Maddie's to sing. They were meant for manufactured all-girl or all-boy bands to sing. And God forbid they should suggest trying one of Freya's. His refusal to even hear the new stuff had been a major cause of Freya getting writer's block.

But there was no way Maddie was going to let him destroy the relationship she had with Freya and Andy. No way.

Freya and Andy came in and sat down on the lounge chairs across from Maddie. Andy raked his hands through his long dark hair and said, "What'd he say?"

Maddie looked at them both and said, "Well, he's not happy."

"When is he ever happy lately?" Freya asked.

"Are we rescheduling?" Andy asked. "Just 'cos, you know, the surf was really good on the coast."

Freya whacked him on the arm and he laughed.

"Well, for starters, we're not going on tour," Maddie said. "The tour company's dropped us."

Andy whistled. "That bad, huh?"

"And we have to make a huge decision," Maddie said. She knew there was no way to sugarcoat it so she just said it. "Dad wants me to go out on my own."

Freya's eyes widened. "Go solo?" she asked.

"Without us?" Andy asked.

"That's what solo is, you idiot," Freya said. She pulled her legs up underneath her, pulled her skirt over her feet, and picked at the hem.

"That is huge," Andy said. He leaned back into his chair and crossed his arms.

"Yeah," Maddie said.

"Are you going to do it?" Andy asked.

"If I don't, we lose the contract," Maddie said simply. "Apparently, dad signed a deal without me a few months ago, and if I don't leave the band at the end of the year to go out on my own, Three's Company loses its recording contract."

"But we lose it anyway," Freya said. "We don't exist without the three of us."

Maddie nodded. "I know."

Andy stretched and folded his hands behind his head. "So what are our choices?"

"We don't have any," Maddie said. "I'm not doing it."

"Wait a minute," Freya said. "So we just walk away from a million-dollar deal?"

"Is it worth it to not sing our own stuff?" Maddie asked.

Andy rubbed his forehead. Business was not his strong point. Maddie knew that. She also knew that he'd play music for free if he had to, but Freya was a different story. Freya would be a harder sell.

"You know Freya's written some more stuff?" Maddie said.

Andy looked over at Freya, who shrugged. "It's not much," she said.

"It doesn't matter," Maddie said. "What matters is it's ours. Not someone else's."

"Maddie's right," Andy said. He got up and walked over to the window. He pulled back the curtain stood for a moment and then turned around. "We got ourselves that deal. We did all our own stuff before, and it was great. We had people who loved our first album. Why can't we do more of that stuff?"

"Because the company doesn't want us to," Freya said. "And they're the ones paying us the money."

"When did it become about the money?" Andy asked.

"When we started making it," Freya replied.

"It shouldn't be about money," Maddie said.

"It's okay for you to say," Freya said. "Your parents are loaded anyway. Andy and I worked hard to get where we are."

"We all did," Maddie said. "That's my point. Look. When I was in Chesterfield—"

"Chester-where?" Andy asked.

"It doesn't matter," Maddie said, waving him away. "When I was away I met this girl, Lizzie. She was mad keen on us. Saw us before we signed the deal. She loved our stuff," Maddie said. "That's who we do it for. Not my dad and not some record company that thinks they know better than we do."

"She's right," Andy said. "If you take the money out of it, we never really liked our last album anyway."

"I guess," Freya conceded. "I still don't understand what we're going to do about it."

Maddie leaned onto the edge of her chair. "We go out on our own."

"What? Quit the company?" Freya shifted in her chair and Maddie knew she'd have a hard time convincing her to walk away.

"Why not? They're threatening to do it to us no matter what we do," Maddie said. "We should call their bluff."

"What about your dad?" Andy asked. "Isn't he going to be pissed?"

Maddie's father was a whole other problem but he was one Maddie would deal with herself. "Do we really need a manager?" she asked. "We didn't have one to start with."

"So what, you're going to sack him?" Andy said.

"Why not?" Maddie replied.

"So, if we do this," Freya said. "Go out on our own, I mean. How do we even start?"

Before Maddie could answer, there was a soft knock on the door, and Jo entered. "Sorry to interrupt," she said, handing Maddie a piece of paper. "I think you should read this."

Maddie skimmed over it and then read it again. She smiled. "I know what we're going to do," she said. "I know exactly what we're going to do."

Andy and Freya asked in unison, "What?"

"We're going back to our roots," Maddie said.

Andy's eyes lit up. "We're going busking?" he asked.

"Not quite," Maddie said. "But I think you'll like it anyway." She turned to Jo. "Can we make it back in time?"

Jo shrugged. "It's doable," she said. "But only if we get started now."

Maddie turned to Andy and Freya. "Are you in?"

"Hell yeah," Andy said. "I don't know what it is, but I'm in."

Maddie and Andy looked at Freya. Freya sighed. "Fine," she said. "I'm in."

"We're back," Andy said, grinning.

Maddie certainly hoped so.

Twenty-four

TESS WAS GIVING BESSIE a brush over and consoling her on missing out on her big moment in the spotlight when Will came and leaned on the fence.

"How are you doing?" Will asked.

Tess shrugged. "Fine. Why?"

"I just thought... it doesn't matter," Will said.

"Just thought what?" Tess asked.

"Nothing," Will said. He kicked at the dirt.

"Did you hear back about that job?" Tess asked.

"Yeah. There was a death in the family or something," Will said. "They're holding over the interviews until January."

"So you still might be in with a chance?"

"I guess," Will said. He scratched the back of his head. "They asked if I wanted to do some volunteer work over the holidays."

"That's great," Tess said. "Are you going to do it?"

Will shook his head. "I told them I had commitments up here."

"What commitments?"

"The festival," Will said.

"What festival?" Tess said. "It's cancelled, remember?"

"About that," Will said. "I spoke to Pop about the festival."

Tess moved around to Bessie's other side, gave her a scratch on her head, and started brushing her chest and front legs.

Will continued. "Lizzie's probably going to kill me for telling you this, but I think you should know."

"Know what?" Tess stopped brushing Bessie and looked up.

"I know you said you already spoke to Pop about turning the festival into a music festival and he said no, but Lizzie and I thought we could give it another shot."

"You went to him without talking to me?"

"I did talk to you, Tess, but you've been so distracted by Maddie—"

"I have not!"

"Yes. You have." Will eye-balled Tess and she eventually had to look away.

"Yeah, okay. So what? What's that got to do with the festival?" Tess asked.

"Nothing. Except you just didn't seem like you wanted to come up with a solution. That's all. And Lizzie and I talked about it and Lizzie said there wasn't a small music festival between Brisbane and Cairns, at least not like we want to do, so we were a prime place to have one."

"They take a lot of organising," Tess said. "That's why Pop said no last time I asked. And bands, good ones, want to be paid."

"See, that's the thing," Will said, walking through the gate and standing in front of Tess. He gave Bessie a scratch on her nose. "All the bands I asked are new ones trying to break into the scene. They all said they'd do this gig for free so they could put it on their website. Get a bit of cred."

Tess didn't say anything and Will continued. "And the other thing is when was the last time Gran and Pop, any of us really, were able to sit back and enjoy the festival? It seems like every year there's more stuff for us all to do to save money. We're so busy working the stalls or on the gate, that we don't get a chance to sit back and just enjoy ourselves."

Tess knew Will was right. She'd actually felt like that last year if she was really honest with herself, but she'd never admitted it to anyone else.

"How's a music festival going to let us enjoy ourselves?"

Will shrugged. "We dial back on the rides and stalls and stuff and concentrate on food vans and bands. Once we do all the setup, there's not much else to do except sit back and make sure it all just runs smoothly."

"So, how did you talk Pop into having it this year?"

"I just asked him to give me one year to prove my point and if it bombed, I'd never ask again."

"And if it works?"

"Then you and Lizzie and I are starting our own music festival." He smiled hopefully, but Tess shook her head.

"I just don't know," she said.

"Look," Will said. "Just see what happens, okay? See how it goes tomorrow and then on Sunday, we'll decide whether we want to do it all again next year."

Tess wished she could be as confident as Will was, but Pop had been right about crowd numbers dropping over the past few years. She had no idea how Will and Lizzie could have organised anything at such short notice but if she believed what Will was telling her, they'd managed it. She sighed. "Fine."

"Great." Will grinned. "But you have to act surprised tomorrow, or Lizzie's going to know I told you. And that could be dangerous for both of us."

"How am I going to act surprised when there are still people setting up?"

"You saw all that?"

"They're in the Big Yard, dope. How can I miss the chip van and the stage trucks?"

"Yeah. Good point," Will said. He rubbed the stubble on his chin and said, "Just pretend I told you that they wanted another night's free camping before they moved on."

Tess had to laugh. "Whatever."

Will gave Bessie a rub on the nose and said, "I should get back to the band. I'll see you in the morning."

Tess followed Will out of Bessie's pen and said, "I should go talk to Pop. I haven't spoken to him in nearly two days."

"Hey, don't let on you know," he said. "Pop thinks it's a surprise for you too."

"Fine," Tess said and headed to the sheds. Even though Will had revealed the secret, it would still be a surprise to Tess if they managed to pull it off.

Twenty-five

TESS PULLED OPEN THE wooden door of the main shed and spotted Pop's feet sticking out from under Chitty. "Pop?"

"Yeah," he grunted.

"What are you doing with Chitty?"

"Putting in a spotlight. So you don't have to use that torch anymore."

Tess walked over to the benches lining the side of the shed. They were covered in grease and oil and red dust, but they were tidy. Pop never left anything on the benches and anyone who worked in there was expected to do the same. If he'd been working on something, an old motor, or bike part, he wrapped it in an old tarp or rag and put it under the bench until he could get to it next time.

Pop said, "Can you see the switch on the dashboard?"

Tess leaned over the steering wheel and spotted the switch Pop was talking about.

"Yeah."

"Turn it on, will you?"

Tess flicked the switch and the spotlight lit up the door in a blinding stream of white light. "You might want to adjust the angle," Tess said. "It looks like it's a bit high."

She watched as the light dropped lower on the door. "How's that?" Pop asked.

"Perfect," Tess replied. She flicked the switch off and Pop pulled himself from under the car and stood up.

"Your grandmother can't complain about you not being safe at night now." He wiped his hands on the front of his coveralls and walked over to the bench to put his tools away in the toolbox. "I cleaned out the filter too, which is something you should do more often if you're going to start driving it again." He pointed at Tess with a spanner before he dropped it in the toolbox.

"Thanks," Tess said. "I'll try to remember."

"I taught you to service it so I wouldn't have to do it myself," he grumbled. He closed the toolbox, shoved it to the back of the bench, and turned back to Tess. He leaned back onto the bench and folded his arms across his chest. "Your grandmother send you out here?"

"Kind of," Tess said.

Pop nodded. Obviously not wanting to talk about what Gran might've said, Pop asked, "Have you been talking to Will?"

"About what?" Tess remembered what Will said and decided to feign innocence.

"The festival."

"I was just talking to him. Why?"

"He came to see me with some harebrained scheme of his."

"Oh?" she said. "And?"

Pop shrugged. "I told him he was dreaming."

Oh, he's good, Tess thought. She decided to test how far Pop would take the lie. "So, all the trucks that are still in the yard. How come they're still here?"

"Buggered if I know. Probably too stingy to pay for a motel I suppose."

"So they'll be gone in the morning?"

"I bloody hope so. They're killing my grass."

Tess tried not to laugh out loud. "So, what are we going to do tomorrow night then, since we haven't got any other plans?" she asked.

Pop shrugged. "Hadn't thought about it to be honest," he said. "Might give your Gran the night off from cooking. Take her out for dinner maybe."

"Right," Tess said.

"Speaking of dinner, you're Gran'll probably have it ready by now. You should get inside and see if she needs a hand."

Afraid that she might let on that she knew what was happening, Tess decided to head inside. As she pulled open the door Pop said, "Tess?"

"Yeah?"

"You know you're my favourite?" Pop smiled.

Tess smiled back. He used to say that to her all the time until she realised that she was his only grandchild. "I know," Tess said.

The sky had gone completely dark and as she walked down the dirt road back to the house, a pair of headlights turned into the Big Yard driveway. Whoever that was, they were late if they were wanting to set up now. Tess wasn't sure why they wouldn't just come earlier tomorrow.

· ♥ · ♥ · ♥ · ♥ · ♥ ·

Tess found Gran in the lounge room, knitting. "Dinner's in the oven," she said, not missing a beat with her knitting needles.

"Thanks," Tess said. As she turned to walk out to the kitchen, there was a knock on the front door. It was unusual because everyone knew to use the back door. Tess opened it and was blinded by a flash of white light. Before she could recover a man said, "Where's Indiana Rose?"

"What?" Tess scrunched her eyes to try to relieve her temporary blindness. The man held out a piece of paper. It took her eyes a minute to adjust but she was horrified to see that it was a copy of the photo that was in the paper that morning.

"Can you confirm that Indiana Rose was staying out here?"

Before Tess could say anything, Gran had appeared at her side. "Go away," she hissed.

"We just want to ask some questions," the man said. He had a pen poised over a notebook.

There was another flash from the camera and Gran stepped forward, threatening the men with her knitting needles. "If you don't get going right this instant, I'll set the dogs onto you."

"But—"

"Go let the dogs off," she said to Tess.

"Okay, okay." The man put his hands up in front of him and backed down the stairs. "We're going."

"And don't come back!" Gran slammed the door and locked it behind her.

"We don't have any dogs," Tess said.

"They don't know that," Gran replied. She pulled Tess into the kitchen and ordered her to sit at the bench. Tess sat on a stool, and Gran pulled a dinner plate from the oven, unwrapped the foil covering, and placed it down in front of Tess along with a knife and fork. "Eat," she said.

Tess was a little worried about what Gran might do if she were to protest, so she did as she was told.

"There'll be more tomorrow, no doubt," Gran said, wandering around the kitchen, putting dishes and cutlery away. She pointed at Tess with a butter knife. "Don't you tell them anything."

"I won't," Tess replied through a mouthful of corned meat and mashed potato. She didn't know what she'd tell them anyway.

"I'll get your grandfather to call Sergeant Collins when he gets in. He'll clear them off quick smart."

"Clear who off?" Pop called from the laundry.

The smell of grease remover drifted into the kitchen and Gran said, "You know I hate it when you wash off inside, Jack."

"The bulb's out downstairs," Pop replied. He sidled up beside Tess and pinched a piece of corned meat from Tess's plate. She swiped at him with her fork and he laughed.

"Gran just fought off some reporters with knitting needles," Tess said through mouthfuls of food.

Pop laughed. Gran huffed and said, "I told them I'd set the dogs onto them if they didn't get going quick smart."

"We don't have dogs," Pop said.

"They don't know that," Gran said and Tess laughed.

"Crafty one, your Gran," Pop said, stirring the cup of tea Gran placed down in front of him.

"Don't you start," Gran said, swatting at him with a tea towel.

Twenty-six

TESS LAY IN BED Saturday morning, listening to the activity going on outside in the Big Yard. She wasn't sure why Lizzie thought she wouldn't work out something was going on, but she'd keep her word to Will and pretend like she didn't know a thing. She was wondering when would be a good time to get out of bed to see her 'surprise' when she got a text from Will.

Heads up. Pretend you're asleep. Lizzie wants to wake you up for the surprise. See you in 5.

Tess lay back and pulled her pillow over her head. She smiled when she heard scuffling outside her bedroom and when the door opened, she resisted the urge to jump up and surprise them.

Instead of the violent shaking that had woken her the day before, Lizzie quietly called Tess's name and gently shook her shoulder. Tess groaned and pretended she was annoyed at being woken up. "What?" she grunted. She opened one eye and looked up at Lizzie who was sitting on the bed. Will was standing in the doorway, holding what looked like a large piece of paper.

"Wake up," Lizzie said. "We've got something to show you."

Tess decided to play it for all it was worth. She rolled over and said, "Go away."

Lizzie said, "Come on, Tess. We've got a surprise for you."

"I don't like surprises," Tess said. She hid her grin with her pillow.

Lizzie pulled the pillow off of Tess's face and said, "If you don't get up, I'm going to get a glass of water and wet you."

Tess rolled back over. "Really? You'd do that?"

Lizzie nodded. Tess realised Lizzie could actually be serious. She sighed. "What?"

"Look," Lizzie said, pointing to Will, who unfurled the paper he was holding. It was a poster.

Tess sat up and rubbed her eyes. "What is that?"

Lizzie jumped up and down on the bed. "It's a poster. For the new and improved Crush Festival. Well, the Crush Music Festival to be exact."

Tess motioned for Will to bring the poster closer so she could see it. 'Crush' was scrawled across the centre of the poster in graffiti type over a blurred picture of a stage with strobe lights flashing down from the top. Around 'Crush' were little graphics that said 'band name here' and in bigger type, under the title, it said 'featuring Major Band'. Right at the bottom, it said 'details to be decided to go here'.

"Obviously it's not finished because we don't know who's coming. But when we know for next year, we can fill in the blanks," Lizzie said. "What do you think?"

She was so excited that Tess found it hard not to be a little excited herself. "It sounds great," Tess said. "I'm not sure Pop will—"

"He's already said yes," Lizzie interrupted. "In fact," she said, looking over to Will. "Will and I have a confession to make."

"About what?" Tess asked.

Lizzie's knee bounced up and down and she said, "We kind of, sort of—"

"We asked Pop if we could do a trial this year," Will finished.

"This year, as in?"

"Today," Lizzie said. She looked at Tess expectantly. "The Crush Festival's going ahead, Tess. As a music festival."

"How did you organise it all at short notice?" Tess asked.

"We managed to talk to Pop before he cancelled the stages and equipment," Will said.

"And," Lizzie said, her eyes widening with excitement, "Will asked a heap of bands to come and play and most of them said yes."

"And we have a special guest coming," Will said.

Lizzie spun around and said, "Shh, don't tell her everything."

"What?" Will shrugged.

"So, what do you think?" Lizzie asked. "Ready to hit the newest music festival around?"

Tess considered just saying yes but decided that giving Lizzie a hard time about it would get her back for being so secretive. She shrugged and said, "I was just thinking of going up to the dam today. Maybe into town, hang out at Piggies'. Music festivals aren't really my thing. You guys enjoy though."

Lizzie's face dropped. "We did this for you," she said.

"Well, you should've asked me instead of going behind my back."

Lizzie looked stricken. "We just wanted it to be a surprise," she said. "The festival's been the best part of living in Chesterfield since forever, and we couldn't just let it get cancelled."

Tess looked over to Will who was trying to hide a smile. He shook his head a little and Tess knew she should just put Lizzie out of her misery. "Fine," she said. "But you have to promise not to go behind my back again."

Lizzie nodded excitedly. "And," Tess said, "you have to let me help you next year."

"Deal," Lizzie said. She hugged Tess so tightly she could hardly breathe. When she let Tess go she said, "Right. Will and I need to go out and help with the bands."

"What do you want me to do?" Tess asked.

"Nothing," Lizzie said. "We've got it sorted. Have some breakfast and come out whenever you want."

"Okay," Tess said.

Lizzie jumped off the bed and pushed Will out the door. She turned and said, "Oh, just so you know, stay away from the main gate in the Big Yard."

"Why?" Tess asked.

"There are photographers and reporters everywhere asking about Maddie and the girl she was kissing," Lizzie said, air quoting 'girl she was kissing'.

Tess's heart sunk. "Oh."

"They don't know it's you," Lizzie said.

"Just stay away from them and you'll be fine," Will said. "See you outside."

Tess lay back on her bed. For just a moment, when Lizzie had been explaining about the festival, Tess hadn't thought about Maddie. But now that Lizzie had mentioned her, she was all she could think about. She checked her phone again, but there were no messages.

She decided to try Maddie one last time. She scrolled through to her number and pressed 'call'. She let it ring and ring and just as she was about to hang up, someone answered.

"Hello?"

"Hello, Tess." It definitely didn't sound like Maddie. The voice was too low. And what was that noise in the background? It sounded like they were on a race track.

"Who's this?" Tess asked.

"It's Jo."

"Oh. I, er, is Maddie there?"

"She can't talk right now," Jo said in her clipped voice.

"Right. Um, well, can you tell her I called? Please?"

Jo sighed. "I'll tell her."

Before Tess could say anything else, Jo had hung up. Tess had no idea whether Jo would deliver the message or not and she wasn't sure whether to feel sad or happy that she finally managed to get through. On the one hand, at least she knew Maddie hadn't lost her phone or broken it or something. On the other, Jo answering the phone meant that Maddie was ignoring her.

Tess put her phone on the bedside table and headed out to get some breakfast. At least one thing was certain, and that was that Will and Lizzie were the best friends anyone could ask for. She really hoped today was a success for them all.

Twenty-seven

"EVERYONE IN?" ANDY ASKED as he pulled his seatbelt across and buckled it.

"Have we got everything?" Freya asked, turning from the front seat to look at Jo and Maddie who were in the back of Andy's van. Squished behind them were their instruments and sound equipment. As much as Andy could fit in anyway. He figured they'd be able to borrow anything else they might need from the other bands when they got up there.

"I think so," Maddie said.

"Right, let's get this show on the road," Andy said. He turned the key in the ignition and there was silence. Freya looked from Andy to Maddie and back again. Before Maddie could say anything, Andy tried again and the van spluttered to life. He laughed nervously and said, "Told you she's still good."

Though they had enough money saved to hire a van, they couldn't get one the size they needed at short notice. They decided that since they were going back to their roots, it would only be right to use Andy's van, just like they used to when they first started gigging. Andy said it was still going well enough to make the six-hour trip to Chesterfield, but Maddie was starting to have her doubts.

She breathed in the old familiar scent of engine oil and cheap air fresheners and smiled. Being in the van brought back so many memories from just a few years ago when they had no idea where they were really heading with the band. She still remembered the day that Andy had turned up with Freya, their old second-hand equipment stacked in the back, and told Maddie he'd got them a gig at a country race day a few hours out of Sydney. They weren't getting paid, except for free accommodation and food, but still, it was an exciting time to actually play in front of people who had no idea who they were yet. Except for having one of their old speakers blow up right in the middle of Andy's guitar solo, the gig hadn't gone too badly. They were asked to do a weekend a month at the local pub, which was a huge flop for the first few months because they were playing to mostly old guys who kept requesting Slim Dusty songs. Even though it wasn't their type of music, Andy loved learning and playing The Pub With No Beer for them whenever they went out.

It was about six months after they started gigging that Freya hit on the idea to record themselves when they practiced and start a YouTube channel, just to see what would happen. If nothing else, they could see how they looked on camera and how they sounded together and make adjustments if they needed to. That had turned out to be what launched their name. For the first few months, they hovered around just ten followers and had no-one following them they didn't know personally. Freya then entered one of their originals into a music competition that was held by a radio station, and though they didn't win, they picked up almost a thousand new followers within a few weeks.

They started receiving requests for covers from fans, which they played, and it was their acoustic cover of Cold Chisel's 'Forever Now' that got them the attention of a record company. On Freya's 18th birthday, they signed a deal with Cherry Studios for the record that would change their lives forever.

Maddie looked out of the van window at the traffic and trees sliding by in a blur. She couldn't pinpoint exactly where things started to change, but it had definitely become a lot harder when they agreed to her father becoming their manager. The first sign really should have been when he started booking them for shopping centre appearances and party gigs. He said they needed to take everything they could get. The more places they played, he'd said, the more people would hear their name. Though that sounded good at the time, Maddie knew they weren't connecting with the people they wanted to with their music.

The tour that Cherry had organised to promote their first record had been the best part of that first year. They played so many little music festivals all over the country it had made their heads spin. It had seemed back then that they were in a different town every day, without too much downtime in between, but they'd all loved it. On reflection, Maddie couldn't help but wonder if that was because her father had stayed at home to 'take care of business'.

They'd arrived back in Sydney after eight months on the road, and after only a week off, Maddie's father had them listening to and deciding on songs for their next album. Freya had written some of her best stuff while they were on the road, but he totally dismissed it. That was the point, Maddie decided, when it wasn't fun anymore. Having her father dictate what they should sing based on business rather than their passion for their music had been the worst thing that could have happened. She'd been so angry at herself for letting him do that to her and to Andy and Freya that she'd finally snapped in Brisbane before they were due to kick off their latest tour.

At the time, she knew she should never have let it go that far, but in the end, she knew it had turned out for the best. After all, she would never have gotten a break as long as she had, and she'd never have met Tess. Tess, who had shown her how to be normal again. Tess, who had helped her realise that friendship and passion and living your own life was what made her happiest.

She wished she could call Tess, just to tell her she missed her, but she'd promised Lizzie she wouldn't. Besides, if she'd heard Tess's voice, she would've crumbled and told her exactly what was happening, just so Tess knew she was coming back and that she couldn't wait to see her.

Maddie lay her head on the window and remembered the first time she and Tess were up at the treehouse, when Tess was telling her about the secret societies and all the fun she'd had up there as a kid. She'd wanted to tell Tess everything then, and she'd so desperately wanted to kiss her, but she didn't want to risk it. Apart from Freya and Andy, Tess and her friends had been the first real people Maddie had met for a long time. The first people to know her as Maddie first and Indiana Rose second.

She thought back to her lunch date with Tess and kissing her in the grandstand. The way the world stopped and how she had to will herself to breathe afterward. How they laughed at tasting like chicken salt and mayonnaise. Snuggling up with Tess at Lizzie's watching movies and forgetting her troubles, even if it was for a short while. Maybe one text wouldn't hurt, she thought. She could just text Tess and say she missed her and that she wanted to see her. She wouldn't give anything away. It would still be a surprise.

She pulled her phone from her pocket, opened a message, and began to type.

Hey Tess. Sorry I haven't text you. I wish I could tell you why but you'll find out soon I promise.

Maddie thought about what she should add next. I miss you too she typed. She read over the message and before she got a chance to send it, there was a loud bang and the van jerked violently sideways. She gripped her phone to stop it from flying out of her hand and grabbed the back of the seat in front of her with her other hand. Andy somehow managed to pull the van over onto the side of the highway without too much more trouble, and they all piled out onto the grass.

"Looks like a flat," Andy said, shifting his cap back on his head and running his hand through his hair.

"You think?" Freya said, pointing to the shredded back tyre. "You've got a spare, right?"

"Of course," Andy said. "But it's under all the stuff in the back."

Maddie walked around to the back of the van and pulled open the doors. "Give me a hand," she said. As she started pulling equipment from the back, her phone rang. She pulled it from her pocket and tossed it to Jo. "Can you deal with whoever that is please?"

Jo caught the phone and headed away from the noise that Maddie, Freya, and Andy were making unpacking the van.

"It's just like old times," Andy said as he started pulling out equipment and placing it on the side of the road.

Freya just huffed as she moved a guitar case over to the grass away from the road.

Maddie sat on the side of the road, her knees pulled up to her chest. "I can't believe you didn't check the spare," she said as Andy started piling equipment back into the van.

"I haven't had to use it in ages," Andy said, grunting as he lifted a drum box into the back and pushed it into place.

"Exactly," Freya said. "God, men can be so bloody exasperating!" She threw her hands into the air and leaned back on the side of the van, her arms crossed on her chest.

"I only checked it like, a couple of months ago," Andy said, wiping his hands on his shorts. "No wait, it was only a few weeks ago. When I was on the coast." He looked up to the sky and rubbed the back of his head. "Oh, yeah. That's right. I got a flat on the way to Byron." He shook his head and laughed. "I knew there was something I had to do when I got home."

Freya punched him on the arm. "I can't believe you didn't get it changed."

"I just forgot," Andy said, looking sheepish.

"Yeah well, we're not going to make it to the festival now, idiot." Freya dropped down onto the grass beside Maddie and sighed.

"The mechanic's on his way," Jo said, coming from the front of the van and shoving her phone back into her pocket. "He's bringing a spare with him and should be here in about half an hour."

Maddie sighed. "I'll have to call Lizzie," she said. "Just in case we're late."

Jo checked her watch and said, "If we get going in the next hour, we should get there with some time to spare."

"I hope so," Maddie said as she waited for Lizzie to answer. She really wanted to see Tess before they had to go on stage.

Twenty-eight

TESS HAD TO PUSH her way through a crowd to get to Gran's baked goods stand. Will and Lizzie had certainly planned the festival out well. The stages were far enough away from the food tents that you didn't have to yell too loud to ask for what you wanted and they'd managed to talk a ride company into setting up a side-show alley with games and rides to keep people entertained away from the music. Tess slipped under the rope at the back of Gran's food tent and stood by the Esky. "How's it going?" she asked.

Gran gave a woman her change and said, "Really good. The cupcakes are almost sold out. I had no idea they'd be so popular." She turned back to serve another customer.

"Do you want a hand?" Tess asked.

"Lizzie and I have it covered," Gran said. "And before I forget, I saved you a cupcake. It's in the esky."

"Thanks," Tess said. She didn't feel like eating though, because she'd just checked her phone for the millionth time, only to discover, yet again, that there were no messages from Maddie. "Are you sure I can't give you a hand?"

"You could go see if Will needs any help," Lizzie suggested. "He's over with the sound guys I think."

"I've already been to see him and there's nothing I can do over there."

"What about Pop?" Gran asked. "Have you seen him?"

"He's gone into town to get some more frozen chips for the Lions van," Tess said.

"Why don't you just go and enjoy yourself then," Gran said. "Lizzie can finish up here in a few minutes and you two can go around and have some fun."

"Yeah," Lizzie said. "I'll meet you over at the clowns."

"Fine," Tess said. She ducked back under the rope and headed over to the games area. On her way over to the clowns, she ran into Will.

"Hey, Tess," Will said. "Enjoying yourself?"

"I guess," she said. "Are you busy?"

"Super busy," he said. "It's amazing how many people are here, isn't it?"

"Any idea how many we've had come through?"

"No idea, but we've had to open up Fitzy's for campers."

"Campers?"

"Yeah," Will said. "There are heaps of people coming from out of town and the motels are booked out apparently. Lucky I mowed the block, hey?"

"Yeah," Tess said. "Very lucky." She didn't think it was luck so much as pre-meditated planning.

"Hey, Will," Lizzie said when she joined them. "We're heading over to Cow Pat Bingo to see who won. You want to come?"

"Are we?" Tess said.

"Yeah," Lizzie said. "I have to take some photos for the paper."

"Sorry," Will said. "I have to go and pick up some more toilets to put on Fitzy's. Have fun though. I'll catch you later."

Lizzie linked arms with Tess, and as they headed to the bingo field she said, "Isn't it great?"

"I guess so," Tess said. The bands they'd had on so far hadn't been too bad, except for that one group whose idea of music was yelling incoherently into the microphone with electric guitars screaming in the background. She couldn't believe how many of the crowd actually enjoyed it.

"Did you hear how many we've had come through?" Lizzie asked.

Tess shook her head. "I just asked Will but he said he didn't know."

"I heard Pop say that we had six hundred as of an hour ago."

"Wow, really?" Tess was amazed. That was double what they'd had last year in total.

Lizzie nodded excitedly. "I know. And they're still coming."

"What did you two do?" Tess asked.

Lizzie shrugged. "All we did was tell a few people they should come, that's all."

"That's all?"

"Yeah," Lizzie said.

When they reached the bingo field, Lonny informed them that Bessie had taken just one hour and twenty-one minutes to pick the winners, which was just short of her record. She'd pooed right on the line between seventy-eight and eighty-eight, which meant that old Mrs Hetherington and her daughter young Ms Hetherington got to share the prize, which was a voucher for Gloria's No Size Too Big Boutique.

As Tess was helping Lizzie organise the two ladies for their photos, a voice boomed from behind them. "You should have someone handing them their prize."

Tess rolled her eyes. Barry Montgomery. She started to say something but Lizzie interrupted. "Sure," she said. "That would be a great idea. Would you like to do the honours, Mr Montgomery?"

"Oh, er, sure," Barry replied as if that wasn't his intention all along.

"As a matter of fact, we should get one with Bessie in the background. Since she was the one who picked the winners."

"Great idea," Barry said, sidling up to Mrs and Ms Hetherington.

Lizzie looked through the camera and said, "Just a little closer. That's it." She took a few shots and then said, "Just a couple more. If you wouldn't mind standing in the middle, Mr Montgomery? Thanks."

Barry adjusted his garish tie and smoothed down his hair as he planted himself between Mrs Hetherington and her daughter, placing his arms around their shoulders.

As she started snapping more photos, Lizzie said, "And just back a little. A bit more."

Mrs Hetherington and her daughter had the good sense to look down as they moved back, but Barry Montgomery, obviously too intent on flashing his winning smile for the camera, did not. The look on his face when he felt his leather shoes sink into Bessie's winning cow pat was priceless. Tess laughed into her hand as Barry cursed and wiped his feet on the grass.

"Got it!" Lizzie said. "Thanks for that. I'll get one of those into the paper next week." She grabbed Tess's hand and pulled her away before Barry could yell at them.

After laughing over the action shots of Barry Montgomery stepping in Bessie's cow pat, Lizzie and Tess decided they needed to eat. The Lion's chip van was doing a roaring trade, and thanks to being the organisers, they slipped around to the back of the van and were able to avoid the crowds lining up at the front.

"His face was a classic," Tess said.

Lizzie laughed. "What about when he did this," she said, pulling a face that captured Barry's shocked expression almost exactly.

Tess laughed. "Do you think your dad will put one of them in the paper?"

"Don't know," Lizzie replied. "But he'll probably blow a couple of the better ones up to put above his desk."

Tess smiled. "I know Pop would love to have one on his dartboard."

"I'll see what I can do," Lizzie said as she shoved a chip into her mouth. "God these chips are so good."

"Uhuh," Tess agreed.

Lizzie had a long drink of water and then said, "Do you miss her?"

"Who?" Tess asked.

"You know who," Lizzie said.

Tess knew exactly who Lizzie was talking about, but she'd spent the better part of the day trying not to think about her. "Yeah, I miss her."

Lizzie nodded. "Have you heard from her?"

Tess dug a chip from the bottom of her cup and scraped some tomato sauce from the side. "Nope." She shoved the chip into her mouth and chewed.

"You really do like her, don't you?"

"What makes you say that?"

"Because," Lizzie said. "The festival is buzzing, Tess, and you've been moping around all day."

"I have not."

"Really? Because that's what it looks like."

"What makes you think it's not because my two best friends were keeping secrets from me?"

Lizzie let out an exasperated sigh. "Because you like surprises, Tess. Both your best friends know that."

"Yeah, well, maybe I don't like surprises anymore."

Lizzie shoved Tess with her shoulder. "I can promise you right now, Tess, that you will love your last surprise. Okay?"

Tess sighed. "Okay. But if I don't like it, you and Will are going to pay big time. Got it?"

Lizzie laughed. "Just trust us, okay? And enjoy the festival like everyone else is."

"Whatever," Tess said.

Lizzie finished off the water in her bottle and screwed the lid on. She tapped on it with her hand and said, "I have a bit of a confession to make."

"Oh God, another one?"

"This one's kind of bad," Lizzie said.

"Oh no. We're not doing karaoke at the festival, are we?"

Lizzie laughed. "No."

"Phew," Tess said. "Nothing could be worse than that."

"Don't be so sure," Lizzie said.

"Come on then," Tess said, digging Lizzie in the leg with her finger. "Out with it."

"You know the picture in the paper? Of you and Maddie?"

"How could I forget?" Tess said.

"Well. That's kind of my fault."

"How? You didn't take the picture. Did you?"

"What? No! Of course not."

"How's it your fault then?"

"I may have put up a photo of you and Maddie together on the blog and someone recognised Maddie."

"Are you serious?"

Lizzie nodded sadly. "I'm sorry, Tess."

"Wow," Tess said. She looked out over the Big Yard. There were people everywhere, dancing, eating, sitting on picnic blankets. It was more people than they'd had over the last few years combined. Tess couldn't be angry with Lizzie over an innocent mistake. Besides, it wasn't like Lizzie knew who Maddie was when she put up the photo.

"Tess?"

"It's okay," Tess said. She turned to Lizzie and put her head on Lizzie's shoulder. "You didn't know, so, forget about it."

"Really?"

"Sure," Tess said. "What was the blog about anyway?"

"Friendship," Lizzie said. "It was about the value of good friends."

Tess smiled. "As long as you only said good things about me," she said.

"I always say good things about you," Lizzie said. Before Tess could reply, Lizzie's phone rang. She checked it and said, "I've got to take this. I'll catch you a bit later?"

"Fine," Tess said. "I'll just go and wander around."

"Enjoy yourself," Lizzie said. She gave Tess a quick hug and then ran off. Tess sighed and as she finished the last of her chips, her phone buzzed in her pocket. She swiped the screen and her heart flipped when a message appeared from Maddie.

Meet me at the treehouse 5 pm.

She checked her watch. 4.45 pm. She'd have to take Chitty to get there in time. Before she headed over to the old shed, she detoured via Gran's tent to pick up the cupcake Gran had saved for her. Or, she realised, the cupcake that Gran had now obviously saved for Maddie. The fact that Gran must have known Maddie was coming back didn't matter, and Tess had to stop herself from running to the shed in her excitement.

Twenty-nine

TESS SPENT THE FEW minutes she had to wait swapping between being nervous and being excited. To get a text out of the blue from Maddie, and to realise that text meant she was back in town was one thing, but to still be wondering whether it was her fault Maddie left was another. Tyres crunched on the gravel outside the treehouse, and Tess took a few deep breaths to calm herself. In reality, it had only been one day, sixteen hours, and around forty-six minutes since she'd last seen Maddie (but who was counting). Tess wiped her sweaty palms on her shorts and found it hard not to fidget. The more she fidgeted, the more her palms sweated and the more she had to wipe them on her shorts. When she heard footsteps on the treehouse ladder, she turned to face the door.

Her heart almost exploded with excitement when Maddie appeared in the doorway, smiling at her. She strode over to Tess and wrapped her in a tight hug.

"I missed you," Maddie whispered against Tess's neck. It sent shivers down Tess's spine.

"Me too," Tess said. "I'm sorry."

Maddie pulled back, holding Tess at arm's length. "You? What are you sorry for?"

"The picture. Of us in the paper."

Maddie shook her head. "That's nothing. Last month they were saying Andy had gotten some girl pregnant."

"Wow."

Maddie shrugged and said, "It comes with the territory, unfortunately."

"I think it sucks," Tess said.

"It does sometimes," Maddie replied. "But the free stuff you get given makes up for it."

"Really?" Tess asked.

Maddie laughed and said, "No, not really." She took Tess's hand and gave it a squeeze. "I want to apologise to you, Tess. For leaving without telling you what was going on."

"That's okay," Tess said. "It's not like we're together or anything."

"Is that what you think?" Maddie asked.

Tess looked down at her feet. They hadn't discussed their relationship and where they stood with each other before Maddie left.

Maddie took both of Tess's hands in hers and said, "Well I don't know about you, Tess

Copeland, but I don't just go around kissing random girls you know."

Tess laughed. "Me neither."

Maddie stepped closer and when she spoke, Tess could feel the heat between them. "I really like you, Tess. And I really, really hope you like me too."

Tess's throat was suddenly dry, so she just nodded.

"Good," Maddie smiled. "I don't know about how things work in Chesterfield, but in Sydney, when one girl likes another girl enough to kiss her, and only her, that means they're, you know, girlfriends."

Tess swallowed. "Okay," she said.

"And girlfriends don't just leave without telling each other why," Maddie said.

"I'm sure it was something important," Tess said, finally able to talk.

Maddie nodded solemnly. "It was," she replied. "But I still should have called you to let you know I was okay."

"So, what was it? Did you get it sorted?"

"I hope so," Maddie said. "The record company wanted us to go in a direction we didn't want to go in. So did my dad. So we quit instead."

"You quit? Can you even do that?"

Maddie shrugged. "We thought about how we were in the beginning before we had a record deal. When we were having fun. It was all our own stuff. Just me and Freya and Andy. So, we decided to just do it all ourselves."

"That's good, isn't it?" Tess had no idea about the music industry and how it worked, but she guessed that if they were happier doing their own thing, then that had to be better than being miserable.

Maddie let go of Tess's hands, walked over to the window, leaned on the ledge, and looked out over the dam. Tess walked over and stood beside her, putting her arm around Maddie's waist. Maddie leaned into her and said, "Yeah. It's good. But it's scary too. We have to produce our own stuff. And sell it. We might not make any money."

"You could always get Lizzie to be your publicist," Tess joked.

Maddie laughed and said, "Funny thing about Lizzie. She emailed me through our website and let me have it about leaving without saying goodbye to you. She said I could make it up to you by coming back to play at the festival. She also asked whether I have a cold because of how badly I sang on Thursday."

Tess laughed. "That sounds like Lizzie."

"So anyway, we announced on our website that anyone who bought tickets to our cancelled concerts could come and see us up here and Lizzie did the rest. She's actually got quite a reach on social media."

"So that's why Lizzie and Will have been so secretive the last few days," Tess said. She shook her head in disbelief.

"You have some great friends," Maddie said.

"Yeah," Tess agreed. "I just wish you'd let me know you were coming back."

Maddie pulled a face. "Sorry. They made me promise not to say anything."

"If I'd known," Tess said, "I would've saved you a cupcake."

Maddie frowned. "Are they all gone?"

Tess shrugged. "Like I said if I'd known..."

"Oh well. Maybe I can have one next time," Maddie said. She leaned her head on Tess's shoulder and Tess breathed in the vanilla scent of Maddie's perfume.

Tess leaned down and spoke softly into Maddie's ear. "I'm just kidding. Of course I saved you one," Tess said, holding the cupcake in front of Maddie. "At least, Gran saved you one. I guess she knew you were coming back as well."

"I suppose it's going to cost me," Maddie said, smiling up at Tess.

"You have no idea," Tess replied. As Maddie leaned in for a kiss, Tess pulled away. "Wait a minute," she said. "I'm not giving the cupcake up that easy."

Maddie's eyes narrowed. "Is that so?"

"Yeah," Tess said.

"All right. What else do you want from me to make you give up that cupcake?"

"A promise," Tess said.

"What type of promise?"

"Promise that you won't leave again without telling me," Tess said. Maddie went to take the cupcake, but Tess pulled it away, just out of reach of Maddie's hand.

Maddie smiled and said, "I can promise that."

This time, Tess didn't pull away when Maddie leaned in and kissed her. Maddie wrapped her arms around Tess's waist and pulled her into her, and it took all of Tess's strength to stay standing. The kiss was soft and sweet, and Tess felt like her heart had melted into her feet.

Someone just outside the door cleared their throat. "Jo," Maddie said. "Great timing, as usual."

Tess laughed.

"I wish I could stay up here with you, but I have to go," Maddie said, nuzzling her head into Tess's shoulder. "I have a concert to put on."

"I don't want to keep your fans waiting," Tess said.

"They've waited a couple of weeks to see us, so another few minutes won't hurt."

As Maddie pulled away, Tess held out the cupcake. "Don't forget this."

Maddie looked at it, seemed to consider it for a moment, and then said, "Hold onto it for later. Meet me back here after the concert? Around nine o'clock?"

"On one condition," Tess said. "You leave Jo at home."

There was a cough outside and they laughed. "I'll see what I can do," Maddie said. She gave Tess another quick kiss and for a little while, after Maddie left, Tess considered just waiting up in the treehouse for the concert to finish. Then she figured that she really should go and watch Maddie sing. After all, that's what a girlfriend would do.

Tess arrived back at the festival in time to see Will's band playing the last song of their set. She found Lizzie waiting at the side of the stage.

"Did you see her?" Lizzie yelled over the music.

Tess nodded. "Thanks," she yelled back.

Lizzie smiled and draped her arm around Tess's shoulders. "What are friends for, right?"

"Right," Tess agreed. She gave Lizzie a squeeze. "You get to see them live. How cool is that?"

Lizzie's eyes lit up. "I know! Isn't it fantastic? And they're giving me an exclusive interview after the show for my blog. And Maddie said she might be able to get it published on a few other music websites she knows about."

"That's great," Tess said. "That's really great."

Lizzie nodded. Pop appeared beside Tess and said, "They've gotten a lot better, haven't they?"

Tess nodded. "Isn't it too loud for you up here?"

Pop turned his head and pointed to the earplugs in his ears and Tess laughed. "Where's Gran?"

"In town at your mum and dad's. She's exhausted after today so she's staying there to get some sleep."

Tess nodded. Pop said, "I just came to tell you I'm heading off as well to stay in town. Have fun, okay?"

Tess nodded and gave him a hug. As he left, Will's band finished their final song with a flourish and the crowd cheered.

Will ran off stage and said, "That was the best fun!"

"You guys were great," Lizzie said.

Will smiled. "Thanks. We're happy to play in front of so many people, but we're not the ones they're here to see."

On cue, Maddie and her band took to the stage to the explosions of pyrotechnics and wild screams of their fans. Maddie looked to the side of the stage and when she saw Tess she gave a little wave. Tess waved back, and Will gave her a poke in the ribs. Tess smiled. She couldn't believe that was her girlfriend standing out on the stage, about to sing to hundreds of people.

Maddie gripped the microphone stand like she'd been doing it all her life, and as the spotlight settled on her she said, "Welcome to Chesterfield!" The crowd screamed. She waited until the noise died down, for the most part anyway, and she said, "Sorry we're late. We had some technical difficulties a few weeks ago, but now we're back."

She pulled the microphone stand closer to her, and as the drummer started playing, Maddie looked back over to Tess and said, "And we're not going anywhere."

Epilogue

TESS FOUND A TABLE in the corner of the uni coffee shop and sat down, dumping her shoulder bag to the floor. She pulled out her notes, placed them on the table, and checked her watch. She couldn't believe that in a couple of hours she'd be done with her first year of uni, and in two days, she'd be back in Chesterfield setting up for the Crush Music Festival and spending some downtime with Maddie. Finally.

The year had been a roller coaster ride of lectures, tutorials, parties with Maddie and Lizzie, and setting up a flat with Will. They'd had mountains of fun looking for furniture at garage sales and second-hand shops, though they had yet to find the coffee tables they were after to replace the cardboard boxes they were still using. Even though it was a pokey little two-bedroom flat, it was set in a triplex and came with a huge backyard where they spent most of their time.

Will hadn't landed the job he'd applied for the year before, but he'd found a casual labouring job with a drummer he'd met at last year's festival which kept him busy. He was also volunteering with Conservation Volunteers and had applied for a short-term contract to help build a walking track in one of the national parks near Chesterfield. He was as happy as Tess had ever seen him, and he'd even started dating a girl he'd met when he volunteered for a project out in Western Queensland a few months back, much to Lizzie's distaste. Though she'd only met her a few times so far, Tess thought Peta was okay. She was a bit of a hippy and a vegetarian, which Tess found amusing since Will couldn't have a meal without eating meat. Will liked her a lot though, and that was enough for Tess.

Lizzie, on the other hand, just thought of Peta as a groupie, and though Tess pointed out that Peta hadn't known about Will's band until after she'd met him, Lizzie wouldn't change her mind. Thankfully they didn't run into each other much, because Lizzie had spent the last year flitting between Brisbane and Sydney, using Will and Tess's flat as a base when she was in town. After the success of the Crush Festival last year, Maddie had asked Lizzie to come on board as their social media guru, and while Lizzie still insisted she wanted to pursue a career as a serious journalist and was studying journalism part-time, she found the offer hard to resist.

Especially when she found out she'd get to tour with the band and help them rebuild their fan base from the ground up. Because of Lizzie and her hard work, Three's Company had picked up a deal with a smaller record company that suited them and their music a lot more than the bigger companies did.

On top of that, Lizzie's blog had been voted in the top ten music blogs of the year, and she'd been turning down offers to write articles for other music sites ever since. Even though Maddie and the band said she could still maintain the blog, Lizzie had decided to give it up since she now had inside information no-one else would have. Though whenever she did have exclusives, her old blog was the first place they were announced. Lizzie was now also the official President of the Official Fan Club and managed a select group of loyal fans, hand-picked by the band, who got access to new music and freebies like shirts and backstage passes for the band's appearances in return for spreading the word about the band on social media. In just over a year, Lizzie had increased the band's fan base ten-fold, and it was still growing.

Though they hadn't been able to see each other much lately, Tess knew that the four of them would be back together at the Crush Festival in a few days. She couldn't wait to get back to the farm to see her grandparents and check out the modifications Pop had made to

Chitty. Despite his initial misgivings on the new direction of the festival, Pop had enjoyed the resurgence. Especially since they didn't have to rely on the council anymore for funding. Despite leaving early last year because of the noise, he'd decided to stick it out this year, which Tess was excited about. He hadn't heard Maddie's band play yet and would get to hear them for the first time. Andy was especially excited. He'd been brushing up on his Slim Dusty songs, just to impress Pop.

Gran was relishing helping Mrs Brannigan in the bakery since they'd become unofficial partners in the business. After Mrs Brannigan had her fall, she didn't know how she was going to keep the bakery open without a qualified baker. Gran had asked a few months before Mrs Brannigan's accident if she could use the bakery to make her now-famous cupcakes because the orders had outgrown her kitchen. It was only natural that she'd taken charge of the shop while Mrs Brannigan recovered after her hip surgery. The cupcakes were sought-after all over the district and tourists dropped in on their way through Chesterfield just to try them, as well as Mrs Brannigan's cream buns.

Tess couldn't wait to get back to her Gran's cooking, and she knew Will was looking forward to it too. No matter how hard he and Peta had tried to teach her, Tess just couldn't get the hang of cooking much else other than spaghetti, though her new favourite meal was pesto pasta. Especially if the pesto came in a bottle. Will hadn't given up on her though, and every Saturday night before they went out, he tried to show Tess how to cook something different. He'd banned Tess from cooking steak after the char grill disaster a few months ago, but she was starting to get the hang of stir-fries. Will said they didn't really count since you just had to cut the veges and toss them in a sauce that came from a bottle.

Tess had managed to impress Maddie with a stir fry the last time she was in town, and Maddie would definitely have told her if it was bad. That was a little over two months ago when Maddie had managed to take some time off after spending months in a studio in Sydney. Things had started to get crazy busy for Maddie and the band around then because they'd finally finished their new album and had started doing interviews and promotional tours to get the word out about it. It had been tough getting used to being the girlfriend of an up-and-coming music star, but thanks to the blurry picture that had made it around the country before last year's festival, no-one was really sure what Tess looked like. It meant that Tess could go to functions with Maddie as her publicist or personal assistant without anyone batting an eyelid, and as long as they managed to keep their hands off each other, no-one caught them out. She knew the time was coming when her identity would eventually have to be revealed before someone noticed them sneaking off to a quiet corner together and getting cosier than an assistant should with her boss. It was general knowledge that Indiana Rose had a girlfriend and that she was from a town no-one had heard about until last year, but Tess dreaded having another photo in the paper of her kissing Maddie, but with a headline like "Rock Star Cheats on Country Girlfriend" or something else just as sordid.

Despite that, Tess still found herself getting overwhelmed at the attention Maddie received when they went out in public, and she found it hard to step back and not get overprotective. Thankfully though, Jo had been a pretty constant companion and had stepped in whenever she needed to. Which was her job, of course, but that didn't make Tess any less grateful for it.

The big bonus for Tess had been getting to know Freya and Andy. They'd all started becoming good friends, and Freya had even been getting knitting tips from Gran. Just last week Gran had sent a package of knitting patterns to Tess to pass on to Freya when she saw her next and she knew Freya would be excited to get them.

And Andy was just about the furthest thing you could get from a spoiled rock star. His favourite thing was to drop into karaoke bars unannounced and sometimes in disguise and belt out one of his own songs. He hadn't been caught yet, and Tess thought that his penchant for karaoke was what had caused Lizzie to fall head over heels for him. Andy had no idea, of course, but everyone else did. Lizzie, being the ultimate professional, desperately tried to hide her feelings, but she wasn't doing a very good job of it. Maddie and Freya had both been doing their best to get Andy to notice Lizzie's affections, without Lizzie knowing of course, but unless it had something to do with music or surfing, Andy was far too clueless to notice much at all.

Tess opened her business law notes and started to skim, and someone in the cafe turned on the radio, just in time for a repeat of the interview Maddie had done last night. Someone said, "Turn it up," and Tess smiled. She'd heard the interview a few times already, but the campus radio was replaying it for the afternoon crowd. She still had an hour before she had to sit for her final exam, so she sat back and listened to it again, just to hear Maddie's voice.

The university radio studio was just like the hundred or so other studios Maddie had been in over the last few months - a small glorified cupboard with electronics equipment stacked wherever they could fit it and wires running all over the floors. There was a small window on one wall where a growing crowd of people was gathering. Maddie gave them a smile and a wave and tried not to think about how many other thousands of mouths had been up close to the same microphone that sat on the desk in front of her. The best thing about this interview was that it was the last one she had to do before she got to see Tess. She wished she could see her tonight, but Tess had her final exam tomorrow and she didn't want to distract her from studying. Tomorrow afternoon, she had a marketing meeting with Andy and Freya and then there was the merchandise they had to sign first thing in the morning so it was ready to send up to Chesterfield in time for the Crush Festival in a few days. She could probably fit in a quick visit but she didn't want Tess to just be a short appointment in her schedule. She'd been so busy with promoting the new album that she was looking forward to a few down days with Tess back at the farm before the festival preparations kicked into gear.

"Ready?" the DJ said, snapping Maddie out of her daydreaming. She nodded. He counted her in and after the introductory music, he said, "Welcome back to BU radio. We're here with the lead singer of the band Three's Company, Indiana Rose. Welcome, Indiana."

Maddie leaned into the microphone and said, "Thanks, Ben. It's great to be here."

"So this last year has been a bit hectic for you and the band."

"Definitely, but I think we've come through it relatively unscathed."

Ben nodded. "A new direction, a new album, and a new management team. A lot of bands would have folded under the pressure. How did you manage to get through it?"

"Freya, Andy, and I just love our music. We wouldn't have given that up for anything."

"But you fired your own dad. How did that go down? Was there like, groundings threatened or anything?"

Maddie laughed. "No, nothing like that. Dad's great at the business side of things and he's actually just come on board as an adviser for us. He just got too involved in the music side of things last time and that took us in a different direction than we wanted to go in."

"So no big family feud then?" Ben raised his eyebrows.

"No. It's all good." Maddie replied. She took a sip of water.

"Great. So tell us about this new direction the band has taken. I don't need to tell you that your second album tanked. Can I say that? That's not too harsh?"

"It certainly did tank and I'm the first to admit it."

"What happened?"

"It wasn't the kind of stuff we'd imagined we'd be playing when we started out in Andy's garage.

We let a lot of outside people influence our choices and it stifled us."

"Anyone in particular?"

Maddie shook her head. "I won't name names. The music business is extremely small, and we still want to sell our records."

"Of course. So no insider gossip. Tell us about the new stuff then."

Maddie shifted in her chair. "We're going back to our roots. Back to when we were busking and sneaking into clubs to gig. We wanted to go back to our acoustic sounds. We really love the raw sounds of fingers slipping over the guitar strings, you know?"

Ben put his hands up. "Now you're getting too technical for me." He held up a CD and turned it over in his hand. "You sent me through a copy of the new album to have a listen to before you came on the show, and I have to say, it's some of your best stuff. If you take your second album out of the equation that is."

"Thanks," Maddie said. "We love it and we've had some great feedback from some of our fans who've had the opportunity to listen to it before anyone else. Freya wrote a lot of it herself, though Andy chipped in with a Beach Boys-inspired ballad. They've both been powerhouses over the last few months, and we've already got a lot of stuff to think about for the next album."

"Wow, that's fantastic. Getting back to this one, which is the appropriately named 'Back on

Track', the official launch is taking place at a new little music festival up the coast. Is that right?"

"That's right. We were invited to a new music festival in Chesterfield called the Crush Festival last year, and the timing was right for us to test the waters on some stuff we'd been playing around with. We had such a great time up there that we've decided to go up again and use it to launch the new album. And we want to hit the bakery while we're there."

"I hear it's fantastic."

"The best," Maddie agreed, smiling.

"We'll have details of the Crush Festival on the website for anyone who wants to get up there." Ben looked up to his producer for confirmation, who gave the thumbs up.

Maddie said, "There are some great bands going up this year. A new rock group called The Trojan Kings will be playing too. They're a crowd favourite since they're local boys."

"Sounds interesting. Talking about Chesterfield, you had another, shall we say, life-changing moment up there? Can we talk about that?"

"Oh yes. Gran's famous cupcakes," Maddie said. "Once you try them, they'll change your life too."

Ben laughed. "That's not exactly what I was talking about."

Maddie smiled and had a quick drink of water. She said, "Sorry, Ben. Yes, I guess we can talk about it, but I'm sure everyone's sick of hearing the story by now."

Ben grinned. "Oh come on now. No-one ever gets sick of hearing a little love story. Can you tell us anything?"

"Only a little," Maddie said. "She's a country girl so she's not used to the spotlight yet."

"Do you get to see each other much?" Ben probed. "I mean, the rumour is that she attends our very own BU City Campus."

He paused and Maddie decided to give him the exclusive was itching for. "Yes, she does actually."

Ben grinned. "You heard it here first. One of our very own BU students is dating a rock star."

Maddie laughed. She promised Tess that she wouldn't embarrass her, but they were getting to the point in their relationship where they probably should be more open about it.

"Getting back to my question," Ben said. "So with you recording and working on the new album and your girlfriend going to uni, there wouldn't be much time in between to see each other."

"It was hard to begin with, but we've worked it out," Maddie replied. "Besides, I think not having me around to distract her lets her study better."

"I wouldn't call love a distraction."

Maddie laughed. "It is when you're trying to study for exams."

"So this is a serious thing then?"

Maddie replied, "Aren't all relationships serious?"

"Not the ones I have," Ben said and they both laughed. "I'm getting the cue to wrap it up. Indiana Rose, it was fantastic to chat with you."

Maddie smiled. "My pleasure, Ben." She relaxed back into her chair and watched as Ben flipped over the CD as he wrapped up the session.

"So, the new album is 'Back on Track', out in a couple of weeks. We're lucky enough to have an exclusive listen to one of the new tracks, 'On the Road', which we'll play straight after the break. You can check out Three's Company on all the usual social media channels, and be listening again to the replay of this interview to have the chance of winning a signed copy of the album."

Maddie leaned forward and added, "And don't forget to check out the Crush Festival up in Chesterfield in two weeks' time."

Ben smiled and said, "For sure. It sounds great. And that's it from me. Tune in next week when we'll be chatting to Matty Hughes from Fox Hole." He nodded to Maddie and she took off her headphones. As she stood up he said, "Thanks so much for that. We really don't get many guests as famous as you on."

Maddie shrugged. "No problem. Any time."

Ben smiled. As Maddie reached for the door handle, Ben said, "Oh, before you go, could you sign my CD?"

Maddie turned and smiled and said, "Sure. Make sure you give it plenty of airplay."

Ben nodded. "Most definitely."

When Maddie finally made it out of the studio after signing other random objects including a coffee mug and two phone cases, she dropped into the back of the car and sighed.

"All done?" Jo asked from the drivers' seat.

"All done," Maddie replied. "Let's get to that meeting. The sooner that's over, the sooner I get to sleep. And the sooner I get to sleep, the sooner I get to see Tess."

·♥·♥·♥·♥·♥·

Tess left her final exam wondering whether she'd actually manage to retain any of the stuff she'd learned that year by the time she started again next year. She was pretty sure she'd passed Info Tech and the business subjects, but Business Law, which she'd just completed, was an entirely different story. With any luck, she'd just scrape through so she didn't have to take a summer class.

As she rounded the corner of the library building, a now-familiar figure in a black shirt and dark jeans stood up from the concrete wall she'd been sitting on. "Hi, Jo," Tess said as she walked past.

Jo fell into step beside her. "How'd you go?"

Tess shrugged. "Okay. I guess I'll find out soon enough once the results are posted."

Jo nodded. "Congratulations on the IT prize," she said. "Professor Ryan was pleasantly surprised I hear."

Tess slowed her pace. "How do you know I got it? It hasn't been announced yet."

Jo shrugged. "I have my ways."

Tess shook her head. She knew she shouldn't be surprised that Maddie's bodyguard was checking up on her. "Has Maddie been asking you to keep tabs on me again?"

"Nope. Maddie doesn't know about the IT prize, or about your intention to change to an Arts degree next year."

"How did you...?" Tess stopped dead. "Why are you checking up on me if Maddie's not asking you to do it?"

"I'm paid to look after Maddie's best interests," Jo said simply. "And technically, you doing well at university is in Maddie's best interests."

"Really?" Tess wasn't sure what to make of that. She guessed she should take it as a compliment.

"You have no idea how much she worries about you when she's away," Jo said.

"Yeah well, I worry about her too you know, and you don't see me asking you to check up on her."

"I get paid to check up on her," Jo said. Tess thought she detected a hint of a smile but she couldn't be sure. She'd never seen Jo smile.

Tess didn't say anything more and let Jo direct her to the rear car park that was kept exclusively for the teachers and academics. As they approached a white four-wheel drive, the rear passengers' side window wound down and Maddie leaned across, a pair of oversized sunglasses shading her face. "Going my way?" she asked.

Tess opened the door and jumped in. She planted a kiss on Maddie's lips and said, "I thought you weren't here for a couple of hours yet?"

Maddie shrugged. "I know the boss. She let me off early. Want to get something to eat? Just the two of us?"

Tess looked across at Jo, who rolled her eyes as she got in and closed the drivers' door. Maddie laughed and said, "Jo can wait outside."

"For sure," Tess said.

As Jo pulled out of the car park and into traffic, Maddie asked, "Did you hear the interview?"

"Five times," Tess replied.

"What did you think?"

"It was good," Tess said. Maddie reached over and put her hand on Tess's leg. Tess took Maddie's hand in hers. "So," she said. "This is serious, huh?"

Maddie pulled her sunglasses down on her nose and looked at Tess. "I wouldn't ditch a marketing meeting for a fling."

Tess grinned.

"So, what do you want to eat?" Maddie asked.

"I could really go for a cream bun," Tess said.

Maddie laughed. "A cream bun it is."

Free short story

Want to know what happens to Tess and Maddie next? You can grab the free short story, 'Maddie and Tess: One Year Later' by signing up to my newsletter at https://bit.ly/crushpb

Acknowledgements

Many thanks to everyone who assisted with the creation of this book. To my cheerleaders and Alpha and Beta readers, Linda Bayfield, Lisa Quinn, Jess 'The Constable' Domrow, Kirstine Hand and Rachel 'Saff' Morgan, your constant encouragement has kept me going during long caffeine-filled nights of rewrites.

To Alison Bedford, who has to be the best English teacher in Australia (if not the world), thank you for picking on my poor sentence structure and grammar early on and steering me in the right direction when I had questions on plot and character. Thank you also for pushing me to get the word count up. Crush wouldn't be the same book without your input. Every writer needs an English teacher in their team.

To my wife, Teresa Brecknell, for putting up with me reeling off random snippets of dialogue and scenes at dinner, and for laughing and crying in all the right places. I love you endlessly.

Finally, to my family and my cousins, who gave me the most wonderful childhood anyone could have imagined. Our real-life adventures on the farm are what fuel my fictional adventures. I love you all.

About the Author

Selena "SR" Silcox started writing sweet romance stories for lesbian teens because she never got to read them when she was younger. She quickly discovered it was a great way for her to relive her glory days from her childhood and make up for all the things she didn't do but wished she could have.

Like kiss cute girls and play professional cricket.

She currently writes the **Girls of Summer Series** of sweet romances for lesbian teens, as well as the **Alice Henderson Series** about girls who play cricket.

You can track her down on Facebook, Twitter, Instagram, and TikTok where she posts updates on her new house, sport, her dogs, and trying to kick her procrastination habit.

www.ingramcontent.com/pod-product-compliance
Lightning Source LLC
Chambersburg PA
CBHW020405120726
47904CB00002B/717